'You don't know me very well, do you, Kim?' Greg said.

'I'm quite sure that we could find a way to work this out.'

'You'll take care not to overplay your hand, won't you?' Kim warned. 'It wouldn't be beyond me to slap a harassment charge on you.'

'Is that so? Still, if you're determined to go ahead with the accusation the least I can do is to give you a frame to hang it on.'

Dear Reader

Wouldn't it be wonderful to drop everything and jet off to Australia—the land of surf, sunshine, 'barbies' and, of course, the vast, untamed Outback? Mills & Boon contemporary romances offer you that very chance! Tender and exciting love stories by favourite Australian authors bring vividly to life the city, beach and bush, and introduce you to the most gorgeous heroes that Down Under has to offer...check out your local shops, or with our Readers' Service, for a trip of a lifetime!

The Editor

When **Joanna Neil** discovered Mills & Boon, her lifelong addiction to reading crystallised into an exciting new career—writing romances.

Always prey to a self-indulgent imagination, she loved to give free rein to her characters, who were probably the outcome of her varied lifestyle. She has been a clerk, telephonist, typist, nurse and infant teacher.

She enjoys dressmaking and cooking at her Leicestershire home.

Her family includes a husband, son and daughter, an exuberant yellow labrador, and two slightly crazed cockatiels.

TREACHEROUS PATH

BY

JOANNA NEIL

MILLS & BOON LIMITED
ETON HOUSE   18-24 PARADISE ROAD
RICHMOND   SURREY   TW9 1SR

For Terry,
Mark and Kerry

First published in Great Britain 1992
by Mills & Boon Limited

© *Joanna Neil 1992*

Australian copyright 1992
Philippine copyright 1992
This edition 1992

ISBN 0 263 77553 4

Set in Times Roman 11½ on 12 pt.
93-9206-42994 C

Made and printed in Great Britain

CHAPTER ONE

THE sound came again—a soft thud, a scuffling, like leaves rustling in the wake of a capricious breeze—and Kim frowned, casting a quick, doubtful glance out of the window into the shadows of the garden. There was little that she could make out in the dim light, except for the dark outline of the shrubbery beneath a ragged canopy of tall trees. How could she tell if anyone was out there? She was not even sure of the layout of the garden. Besides, the unsettling thought whispered along her spine, hadn't the noise been louder this time, as if it had come from within the house itself?

Kim shook her head, the honeyed strands of her hair moving in a silken swath about her face. Of course that was not possible. Apart from herself, the house was empty. She was on edge, that was the trouble. Late at night, alone in a strange house, it was not surprising that her mind was playing tricks on her, magnifying the slightest creak of floor-boards, allowing the clanks and mutterings of the heating-pipes to turn to monsters in her head.

She resolutely turned her back on the window. She had finished what she had come to do, and now she could leave. Leaning back against the smooth grained wood of the work-top, she surveyed the kitchen with rueful appreciation. Coulter had unerring taste, she'd give him that. No expense had been spared on this place, she judged, from what she had seen so far.

A sudden muffled scraping sound had her jerking to attention, all her senses on alert. Someone was in the house. An intruder, someone who knew that Coulter was away—and was creeping with stealth through the rooms on the ground floor. Why had the alarm not gone off? Her thoughts whirled in confusion, her heart thumping erratically. Standing very still, she held her breath and listened. Nothing. Everything was quiet. She was imagining things.

Slowly, her lungs began to work again. Perhaps it was because the house was set back from the road in splendid isolation that she was getting the jitters. It would be all too easy for a burglar to creep through the grounds without being seen, and Coulter's home would certainly prove a treasure trove for anyone so inclined. That was one of the reasons he had Steve keep a regular check on it whenever he had to go away.

She would not let herself be spooked. She had helped Steve out, and now she was going—back to the warmth and comfort of her own flat.

Snapping off the light, Kim walked out into the hall, pausing momentarily to accustom herself to the gloom. There was a switch somewhere, but the silvery beams of moonlight beckoned, filtering through the small panes of glass set in the solid mahogany of the front door.

She started forward, carefully, but, even so, she was totally unprepared for the shocking swiftness of the attack when it came. Her arm was caught in a grip of steel, she was swung round in a sudden, violent move that knocked the breath from her lungs. The shadows leapt, the air was alive with malevolence, sending shivers of fear shooting along her nervous system.

Instinct took over, and she aimed a kick at her hard-boned assailant, hearing it connect with a satisfying crack. The man gave a muttered oath, and she followed up her advantage with a swift chopping motion of her elbow, feeling the blow reverberate along her forearm. His hold loosened a fraction, and she wrenched herself free, making for the door.

She did not reach it. Fingers closed on her arms like a vice, dragging her back.

'Not so fast. You don't get away that easily.'

A scream broke in her throat, cut off as she was slammed backwards with devastating force, and the compelling weight of a hard-muscled, lean body drove her painfully against the wall, her shoulders ground beneath the powerful lock

of his arm. His free hand moved, there was the
click of a switch, and light flooded the hall.

Startling blue eyes, chips of ice from a frozen
pool, skated over her. She read the dangerous,
determined glitter in those cold eyes and made a
desperate attempt to struggle free.

'Keep still, lady. You're not going anywhere.'

His voice was low and gritty, deadly with
intent. Kim had no doubt he meant to enforce
his words. Trapped by the solid bar of his arm,
she was powerless to move as he brought his other
hand up, the fingers travelling to curve against
the slender column of her throat. Panic welled
up in a stifling wave that threatened to over-
whelm her until she came to her senses and
clamped down on it sharply, cold outrage
creeping in its place.

'Take your hands off me,' she said through her
teeth.

His jaw clenched, a muscle flicking with the
action. He said coolly, 'You're hardly in a position to make demands.'

The words chilled her to the bone. She studied
him warily from beneath her lashes, disturbed by
the tough, chiselled lines of his face, the firm,
unrelenting mouth. She felt the pressure of his
arm pinning her inexorably to the wall. He did
not intend to let her go.

She willed herself to think coherently, to form
some plan of action. His height alone was intim-

idating, but the controlled strength with which he held her was only the tip of the iceberg, and the knowledge of what he could do to her filled Kim with terror. She had disturbed him rifling the house, and perhaps tomorrow, or the next day, someone would come along and find her lifeless body. The picture that conjured up was enough to drive her into reckless action.

Small beads of perspiration broke out on her brow. Tensing, she caught her breath and brought her knee up in a sudden, swift arc, but his reflexes must have been second to none, and this time she was out of luck. He reacted with lightning speed, knocking her leg sideways with his own in a blow that made her cry out.

Stunned by his unexpected retaliation, she stared up at him, her eyes smarting with mingled fear and frustration. She had tried, and failed, and now there was the ominous threat of retribution hanging in the air between them.

'That was a bad move,' he informed her unpleasantly, anger tightening his features and adding dark emphasis to the harsh planes and angles of his face.

She swallowed painfully against the dryness of her throat, but she could not give up all hope; there had to be some way she could fight him.

'What did you expect?' she said, tilting her chin, her mouth jutting in defiance. 'I'm warning you—try anything with me and you'll get more than you bargained for.'

The soft challenge in her voice seemed to amuse him. His hold on her loosened slightly, and he brought his hand up to feather with mocking disregard along the line of her jaw.

'Really?' he murmured. 'What did you have in mind?'

She bit him then, hard, her teeth sinking into the long finger that had dared transgress too close.

He jerked his hand away with a curse that turned her ears pink, but he did not move back and she was still caught in the prison made by his long-limbed body. Damn him, the man was a fiend.

'Let me go,' she rapped, desperation bringing heated colour to her cheeks.

'Forget it,' he growled. 'Tell me what you're doing here.'

'Trespassing on your patch, am I?' she queried with silky intonation. 'Isn't that too bad?'

'For you, yes,' he rasped, his white teeth bared in a snarl. 'I want to know precisely what you're doing in my house, and I'm warning you, the explanation had better be good.'

His house? Kim's throat closed in dismay, a pulse beginning to throb violently at her temple. How could she have known that this was Greg Coulter? What was he doing here? He was supposed to be in Europe until the middle of next week, wasn't he?

She stared at him, dumbfounded, her grey eyes wide and searching.

'Something happen to your tongue?' he gritted, snatching up a bunch of her hair in his hand and winding it around his fingers. He pulled at it, dragging her face upwards, closer to his. She tried to draw back.

'You're hurting me,' she protested, as her efforts to twist away from him came to nothing.

'Then stop struggling and answer my question,' he said without sympathy. 'Why are you here?'

'What do you imagine I'm doing?' she muttered. 'Do you think I came to raid the place?'

'That thought had crossed my mind,' he agreed drily, much to her annoyance. 'You tried to run. That speaks for itself of a guilty conscience.'

'Do you always attack first and ask questions later?' she retorted. 'You scared me half to death. What was I supposed to do? I didn't stop to think.'

His mouth made a cynical line. 'And I suppose if you had, you'd have told me you were here to do a little thieving.'

Kim stiffened. 'A little? Why put a limit on it? After all, your house is full of treasures that I might take a fancy to. You should have given me longer. I could have brought the van and cleaned you out.' Her voice was laced with heavy sarcasm.

'As it is, I'm practically festooned with your belongings.'

She didn't like the way his blue eyes glinted at that. 'Are you?' he murmured, releasing her hair at last. 'In that case, maybe I should make a search.' His gaze moved with deliberate provocation over her slim figure, taking in the softly clinging woollen sweater, and the smooth-fitting skirt that skimmed her hips.

Frostily, she said, 'I wouldn't advise it.'

He gave a soft laugh. 'Wouldn't you? But then, you don't know me, or you'd know that I don't always follow advice.'

Kim's grey eyes narrowed. She remarked coldly, 'Your arrogance is incredible.'

'You don't suffer from a shortfall of that yourself,' he threw back at her. 'You're forgetting that this is my house, and I have every right to call the police and have you charged.'

'Go ahead,' she told him, her mouth tight. 'You're so quick to jump to conclusions, you deserve to have egg on your face. I'll have my list of counter-charges ready, shall I?'

He scowled at her. 'How did you get in?'

Kim's look was scathing. 'The window might have proved a little tricky for me in this skirt, so I decided to use a key and come in through the front door.'

'You're lying.' The blue eyes bored into her accusingly.

Kim shrugged. 'OK. If that's the way you want it. I saw a window open round the back, and I shinned up a drain-pipe until I could just about——'

'Let's do without the fairy-tales,' he cut in. 'Show me the key.'

She reached into the pocket of her skirt and drew out the small brass key, holding it on the flat palm of her hand.

He took it from her. 'Where did you get this?' he demanded.

'From Steve. You gave it to him, remember, so that he could look over your house whenever you had to go away.'

Coulter's face hardened. 'Don't you mean that you persuaded my secretary to hand it over?'

Kim's temper rose in a swift, stormy tide. She resented his constant implication that she was lying. 'I mean exactly what I say. Steve asked me to do him a favour, and I agreed. Why on earth should I want to contact your secretary?'

'Because I left instructions for her to get the key back.'

The cold anger threading his voice alarmed Kim. Had something happened that she did not know about? She worried at her lower lip with her teeth, drawing back on her memory to dredge up any clue, but without success. When she had called at her mother's house last week, there had been no indication that anything was wrong, and she had gone on to her three-day conference with an easy mind. Now, though, judging by Greg Coulter's icy expression, it looked as though she'd come back and stepped right into a hornets' nest.

'I didn't know that,' she said, frowning.

'How remiss of Bennett not to tell you,' Coulter remarked tartly. 'I dare say he gave you clear enough instructions of what to look for once you were in here.'

'I don't know what you're talking about,' Kim said with an exasperated grimace.

'How convenient.' Coulter's mouth curved unpleasantly. 'What's your connection with Bennett?'

Her head came up at his tone. 'He's my step-father,' she said coolly.

'Ah.' Coulter gave a brief nod. 'That explains a lot.'

'Does it?' Her brows came together fleetingly. 'I'm glad one of us has seen the light. Why don't you share your great wisdom?' She stepped backwards, away from him, her eyes full of scorn.

In the next instant, his hands had shot out to grip her, dragging her towards him, and she began to regret that short-lived moment of flippancy. He said slowly, 'I should take care if I were you. That sharp tongue of yours is going to land you in a lot of trouble before long, and I warn you, my patience is on a very short fuse.'

'Tell me something new,' she muttered under her breath. His proximity was having an unnerving effect on her pulse-rate. His hands spanned her waist, his thumbs resting lightly beneath the swell of her breasts, and she wondered distractedly if he was aware of the erratic pounding of her heartbeat.

She hated him for making her feel this way. He had done nothing but goad her, and throw accusations at her, when all she had done was misguidedly try to help out by looking over his house.

She jerked away from his grasp. 'I was trying to do you a favour,' she said huskily. 'Steve was bothered that the weather might change for the worse over the weekend when he couldn't make it down here, and he was right, wasn't he? I switched the heating to a low setting, just to keep the chill off the water-pipes.'

'That sounds very commendable,' he said with a cool twist to his mouth. 'Except that it also provides an excellent excuse for getting into the house. What came next on the agenda—a swift search through the bureau, or a quick riffle through my desk?'

Kim clenched her teeth angrily. 'I wish I'd left it switched off, and broken the control panel,' she asserted fiercely. 'Nothing would give me greater pleasure than to have your pipes break and your belongings float off to join the nearest river.'

'Prone to flights of fancy, are you?' he murmured silkily, and she glowered at him with deep dislike.

'I'm beginning to develop elaborate ones where you're concerned,' she snapped.

His smile mocked her. 'It's...interesting...that I should feature so much in your daydreams, after such a short acquaintance,' he said in a low drawl, and she ground her teeth together painfully. 'But,' he went on, 'you don't need to concern yourself about me any longer. I shall see to my own domestic affairs from now on.'

Tight-lipped, she said, 'Of course. You rushed back specially from Europe to see to your central heating. I can see that air travel for you is going to become as automatic as hopping on a bus.'

His gaze shifted over her. 'In fact,' he said, 'I returned to England the day before yesterday.' Seeing her puzzled expression, he added, 'I stayed on at my penthouse suite to clear up some pressing business matters. I'm sure Bennett must have realised I should not be returning home for a while, but somewhere he made a slight miscalculation.'

Kim's eyes narrowed at the gibe. 'I have no idea what you mean, but, as you're so obviously in command of the situation, I'll take my leave of you.' She walked to the door. 'Goodbye, Mr Coulter. Don't bother to thank me, will you? I won't say that it's been a pleasure.'

She lifted a hand to open the door, but he halted her, his palm flat on the polished mahogany. 'You have the advantage over me—I don't know your name.'

'That wouldn't do, would it?' she remarked tautly, knowing that she would not get past him without this final submission. 'It's Darby, Mr Coulter—Kim Darby.'

He let her go, but she had time to register the slight drawing together of his dark brows before she went out into the cold air. Had he recognised the name?

The import of what she had done began to cloak her senses with apprehension as she made her way towards her car. How could she have let him rile her that way? She had so much to lose, yet she had allowed her temper to get out of hand. Coulter had not known who she was—he had not been in England when she had been interviewed by the personnel department—but when she returned to work on Monday morning he would find out soon enough.

It did not bode well for her. She bit her lip as she slid behind the wheel of her car and turned on the ignition. It was all his fault, but she had behaved like an idiot. Her cheeks filled with heated colour. For heaven's sake, how many women began their relationship with the boss by using their knee as a lethal weapon?

CHAPTER TWO

THE thought that she could well be out of a job by the end of next week gave Kim more than a few qualms throughout the following day. She ought not to have let him goad her—that was the crux of the matter. She had far too much to lose.

Coulter Construction was the leading light in the area. Wasn't that why she had jumped at the chance to apply for the vacancy in his architects' department? The experience would have been an invaluable step up in her career, but now she had probably blown it.

If only the man at the top could have been anyone but Coulter. He was insufferable. It was small wonder she had lost her cool, she reasoned as she set to work to clean her small flat. What was she supposed to have done when he attacked her? Submitted meekly? Never.

She turned on the taps, hearing the heavy fall of water gush into the sink. All right, so she had been in his house, and he had felt justified in concluding that she had broken in. Fair enough. Maybe it was a logical assumption to make, she admitted grudgingly. But he had hardly given her a chance to explain, had he? And then, when she had begun to tell him the truth, the man had the nerve to call her a liar. She scowled. Mean, moody and downright suspicious—didn't that just about sum him up?

His hard, arrogant features stole into her mind, pushing violently to the forefront of her consciousness, invoking all kinds of unsettling thoughts. The vision of that strong, angular jaw had her fingers curling into a small fist, itching to make contact. The nose had no business to be so straight, anyway. And whoever had such piercing blue eyes? Just remembering their fierce scrutiny had her fidgeting.

She blinked, and returned to her scrubbing of the sink with renewed vigour, making a determined effort to shift him from her mind. The man was totally despicable. But then, she supposed, he hadn't reached his position in life by being agreeable. Why was she allowing him to provoke her this way?

By evening, the flat had been restored to its customary neatness, and gleamed faintly from her efforts. Kim surveyed it with satisfaction. After she had made herself something to eat, she would pay her mother and Steve a short visit. They should be back from their trip by now, and perhaps they could throw some light on Coulter's strange attitude.

Maureen and Steve were sitting by the rugged pine table when Kim walked into the brightly lit kitchen later that evening. She greeted them cheerfully, asking, 'Did you have a good holiday?' Giving her mother a quick smile, she added, 'I've brought your prescription with me.'

She placed a small package on the table, and studied her mother's face with a slight frown. From the sallowness of her complexion, she judged that Maureen was just about due for her visit to the renal unit at the local hospital.

'Thanks,' her mother said gratefully, slipping the two pill bottles into a drawer. 'It was fine. It made a lovely change.'

Kim accepted the comfortable answer, but she was more than a little disturbed by the unnatural shimmering of her mother's cornflower-blue eyes. She glanced at Steve, who stood up and went over to the sink, reaching for the kettle.

'Your mother needed a break,' he said, and Kim nodded. Of course, ideally, an operation would be the answer, but until that became possible Maureen had to rest as much as she could and try to keep up her strength.

At least the journey to the hospital for treatment was not so long and tiring these days. Steve had thought hard about what he could do to ease his wife's debilitating condition. Hospital funds had been tight, and there was a waiting list for home dialysis units, so in the end he had decided to move them to a house that was much closer to the hospital. Kim did not doubt that it had been a difficult decision to take, knowing the state of the housing market and the high interest rates prevailing, but despite the cost Steve felt it had been worth it, she was sure. It had done a lot to take some of the exhaustion from her mother's features.

Steve filled the kettle, replacing it on its stand, and Kim noted the fine lines of tension drawn across his face. She said casually, 'You were both due for a holiday. From all the overtime you've been putting in lately, I was beginning to think you must have shares in the company.'

Steve sucked in his breath, and Maureen gave a brittle laugh. 'There's not much likelihood of that.'

Kim raised a brow, and her mother went on, 'He gets few enough thanks for all his hard work. All Coulter is interested in is getting the job finished as soon as possible so that he can make a quick profit. People don't matter to him. They can fall by the wayside once he's had his money's worth.'

'You sound bitter,' Kim murmured reflectively. She looked from one to the other. 'Is something wrong? Have I missed anything?'

Maureen shot a glance towards her husband, but stayed silent. Steve's face was shuttered as he began setting out cups on the table. When he finally spoke, it was with an odd, flat tone to his voice that stirred Kim's feelings of apprehension.

'You were at the conference in Nottingham when Coulter arrived back. No one expected him. It was completely out of the blue. There didn't seem to be anything untoward about his return at first, and we just carried on as normal. Then he had a meeting with our main client—Alan Masters.' Steve's hazel eyes flickered, and he straightened. 'Apparently, Masters was dissatisfied with the way things were going on site. It seems he had a list of complaints as long as your arm, and he wanted to know what Coulter was going to do about it.'

Kim frowned. 'What sort of complaints—structural defects? Labour costs?'

'No,' Steve said, 'nothing like that. As far as I can tell, he objected to some of the materials that were being used in the construction.'

Kim's brows came together in a thin line. 'Was there something wrong with the materials—anything likely to cause problems?'

'I don't think so. We might have substituted some products with those of alternative manufacturers—there's often very little to choose between them as far as quality goes, but there might be difficulty with availability, or perhaps a slight difference in price. Whatever we decided wouldn't affect the work. Coulter's very particular about how things are done. But it seems that Masters is being finicky and wants a lot of things changed.'

Steve sat down, his body sagging with weariness. He ran a hand through his brown hair and went on, 'Coulter promised he would investigate, and after Masters left he called me into his office. He questioned me for half an hour or so.' He paused, his face very pale. 'The upshot of it is I've been suspended.'

'You've what——?' Kim gave a gasp of disbelief, staring at him in bewilderment, then shook her head. 'No. That can't be true——'

'It's true enough,' he insisted tautly.

'But it doesn't make sense,' Kim persisted. 'Why on earth would he do that? I don't understand—surely you've done nothing wrong? You've always been the linchpin of the business. What reason could he have for treating you this way?'

'I'm the contracts manager,' Steve said wearily. 'Someone has to take the blame if things go wrong.'

Kim could not let it go at that. 'You know your job,' she said firmly, 'and he's always trusted you to run things properly. How can he make an instant decision like that? If things aren't to Masters's liking, surely they can be put right?'

Steve's shoulders moved in a gesture of defeat. 'Masters talked of people getting backhanders, doing deals, said he wasn't doing business with us any more unless Coulter took action. So that's what he's doing. When all's said and done, the customer has to be placated. I was in charge of the site, so I have to take responsibility.'

'He gets to shoulder the blame, even if it wasn't his fault,' Maureen put in stiffly, her fingers twisting and untwisting in tense little movements. 'Steve wasn't in on this contract from the beginning. Another manager dealt with everything.'

Kim looked from her mother to Steve. 'Is that true?' she asked. 'Was someone else in charge?'

'I took over from another man,' Steve confirmed. 'He's working abroad now, on a long-term contract. I doubt there's much likelihood of getting in touch with him. From what I gathered, he'll be travelling about a lot.'

'But didn't you say all this to Coulter?'

'I think so—yes, I must have done—but things got a bit heated. I'm not sure that he listened.'

Kim's mouth made a grimace. That sounded exactly like the Coulter she had crossed swords with. 'He has to listen—that's your proof, isn't it?' she said urgently. 'I mean, any documentation would have been signed by the other man; you wouldn't have been involved in any way.'

'I don't know where any of it is,' Steve muttered. 'Coulter went through my office like a hurricane. The place is bare now—no paperwork in there, nothing.' His mouth moved jerkily. 'I don't know what he thinks he'll find. When all's said and done, though, it doesn't really make any difference to the outcome. I've been suspended to keep Masters sweet, and it looks as though I'm finished now.'

'Are you certain there's no other reason behind all this?' Kim asked with a frown. Much as she disliked her new employer, she had to turn over every possibility. She couldn't help remembering

Coulter's accusations that she had been searching his house.

Steve shook his head. 'It's all come as such a shock, I don't know what to think any more.'

'He's being used as a scapegoat,' Maureen said. 'There isn't any other explanation, is there? You'd think, after all these years with the company, loyalty would count for something, wouldn't you? He started with the firm long before Coulter came to take over. He's probably forgotten more than that man ever knew. It isn't fair, the way he's being treated.' Her eyes misted, filled with despair, and Steve reached over and pressed a hand gently to her shoulder.

'Don't upset yourself,' he said quietly. 'We'll work things out, you'll see.'

'But I don't know what we can do,' she said, her voice muffled by tears. 'How will you find another job at your age? Who will take you on? We'll have to sell the house, rent somewhere. I don't know what's going to happen.'

'Nothing bad's going to happen,' Kim murmured soothingly. 'Steve's right; we'll get this sorted out. He wasn't responsible; it was the other manager who caused all the trouble, and Coulter will come to see that.' She would make sure of it.

She lifted her gaze from her mother's troubled face to Steve. 'I thought you always kept a notebook of any transactions you made—you were always jotting things down in it after you had finished work for the day. Wouldn't that help?'

Steve's attention was on Maureen. 'I'd forgotten about that,' he muttered distractedly. 'I doubt it would be any use.'

'Where do you keep it?' Kim asked. 'May I look? Perhaps I could borrow it; I might be able to come up with something.'

'The bureau,' he said. 'Help yourself, but I don't think it will do any good.'

Kim went over to the cabinet and flicked through the contents while he turned to Maureen once more.

'Why don't you go and rest for an hour or so?' he suggested softly. 'You'll feel much better when you're not so weary.'

With a small sound of relief, Kim found what she was looking for, and concentrated her attention on the well-thumbed pages of the notebook. 'It's full of day-to-day business dealings,' she said after a while. 'I'm sure it will help.'

She looked at her mother's tired, anxious face, and felt a knot form in her throat. This was all Coulter's doing. If Maureen had a relapse she would lay the blame squarely at his feet.

'Do as Steve says,' she murmured, slipping the book into her pocket. 'I shall have to go now, but I'll stop by tomorrow to see if you need anything.'

After she had seen Coulter, she added silently to herself. He was not going to get away with putting another man's wrong-doings on to Steve. If he had not been prepared to listen to her stepfather, she would make certain that he heard what she had to say. She would not allow him to upset her mother this way and destroy her health. Her lips firmed. Greg Coulter would find he'd bitten off more than he could chew if he tried to tangle with her. She might be a mere woman, fighting in a man's world, but she wasn't afraid of him—job or no job—and one way or another he was going to get his come-uppance. She would see to it.

There was hardly any point in telling Steve and her mother what she planned to do. It would only give them further cause for worry.

Instead, she said on a hopeful note as she left, 'It will probably turn out to be a storm in a teacup, you know. Steve has always been the company's right-hand man. Coulter can't let him go without completely gumming up the works. As Steve said, he's just doing it to keep Masters happy. Once this blows over, everything will go back to normal, you'll see.'

Her words were meant to be soothing, and, from the slight relaxation in her mother's features, Kim knew that they had had some effect. Not for one minute did she actually believe what she had said. It was clear that Steve was troubled by the whole business, and having met Coulter herself and suffered at first hand from his ill-founded accusations she could well see the cause of his despondency. Something had to be done, and quickly.

It was ten o'clock Monday morning when Kim walked briskly through the vestibule of Coulter Construction and headed for the lift that would take her up to the prestigious offices of the building. There had been no lessening in her resolve to confront him. In fact, the more she had thought about it, the more her determination had grown.

She had stayed at her desk that morning only long enough to deal with some urgent business, chafing all the while at the delay. Even the slow pace of the lift as it slid upwards grated on her nerves, and when the doors finally swished open she strode impatiently along the carpeted corridor to his secretary's office.

The girl was obviously startled as Kim burst in through the door, disturbing the hushed and sacrosanct atmosphere of the higher echelons.

'Can I help you?' she said, recovering quickly, and giving Kim a polite smile.

Kim's glance swept her, taking in the stylish cut of her plain black dress, the shining auburn hair, and large violet eyes. So he liked to surround himself with good-looking people, did he? She might have guessed.

'I want to see Mr Coulter.'

The girl looked doubtfully at the diary on her desk. 'Do you have an appointment? I don't recall...'

'No, I don't, but I need to talk to him.'

'I'm afraid that isn't possible right now.' The auburn hair swirled lightly as she bent to finger through the pages of the diary. 'Perhaps you'd care to make an appointment—he's been away for some time and there are a great many matters needing his attention. We may be able to slot you in towards the end of next week.'

Her mother's distress cut across Kim's thoughts and made her more determined than ever to get the matter settled here and now.

'Next week will be too late,' she said with precision. 'What I have to say really can't wait.'

Making for the inner door, she flung it open and pushed her way into his office, ignoring the girl's horrified cry of, 'But you can't go in there...'

Greg Coulter was seated behind his desk, leafing through a file with frowning concentration. He picked out a document and looked up as Kim marched in, his cool blue eyes flicking over her.

His secretary said, 'I'm sorry, Mr Coulter—she wouldn't make an appointment—she just walked right in...'

Her voice faded. Coulter's glance skimmed over the paper he was holding.

'An unfortunate tendency with Miss Darby, I'm afraid,' he replied drily. 'She doesn't seem to care much for invitations.'

'I want a word with you,' Kim mouthed tightly.

The girl hesitated in the doorway, uncertain. He gave a slight nod. 'It's all right, Mandy. You can leave us.'

As Mandy withdrew, pulling the door closed behind her, he turned his attention back to the paper in his hand as if he had never been interrupted. Kim glowered at the top of his head, several choice epithets forming on her lips. She bit them back. If making her wait was a tactic he was using, she was not about to fall into his trap.

He looked very different today from how she had seen him before. This was his lair, his stalking ground, and the clothes were part of it. His suit was formal, waistcoated, dark grey, the expensive cut of the cloth underlining the powerful image of a successful businessman. It emphasised the broad shoulders, the lean, taut-muscled body. His shirt was crisp, the cuffs picked out with gold links, the colour of the thin stripes echoed in his tie.

He continued to study the document for a moment or two, his dark brows drawn together. Then he placed it on the polished surface of the desk and took a pen to write across it in a bold black script.

At last he looked up at her, his face hard-boned, ruthless, his expression giving nothing away.

He leaned back in his seat, watching her, taking his time. Kim stiffened. She felt the shift of those brilliant eyes as they travelled over her. Her tailored suit, ideal for the office, she had thought, was no protection. Cut in a classic style, she wore the jacket open, the lapels of her cream silk blouse a vivid contrast to its rich burgundy tones. The skirt tapered smoothly to mid-calf, to give a glimpse of long, shapely legs, her slender feet encased in stylish leather stilettoes. Under Greg Coulter's glinting appraisal, she was uncomfortably aware that she might just as well have worn nothing at all.

She would have liked to say something sharp and pithy, but that was what he wanted, what he was waiting for, and she wouldn't give him the satisfaction. She lifted her chin, the line of her jaw accentuated by the way her hair was pinned, lifted in an upswept style. There was obduracy in the gesture, and more than a hint of stubbornness in the full pink mouth.

'Well, Miss Darby,' he said, his voice deep and incisive. 'Perhaps you'd care to explain what has prompted this visit?'

She was still smarting from his insolent inspection, and the look she gave him was withering. 'Don't kid yourself,' she advised him shortly. 'It isn't your fatal attraction.'

'I'm glad to hear it,' he drawled, one corner of his mouth twisting in lazy acknowledgement. 'It would be tedious to have to throw you out.'

'Shall we dispense with the small talk?' she gritted.

'Please do,' he agreed coolly. 'I have a busy schedule. I'd appreciate it if you could get to the point.'

'I'm sure you know very well why I'm here,' Kim seethed. 'I can't imagine how you could even contemplate getting rid of a man who's always given his very best for this company.'

Coulter frowned. 'Sit down, won't you?' he suggested, indicating a chair. He rested the palm of one hand on the table, absently drumming his fingers on the wood. 'Are we talking about Bennett?'

'How many others do you have lined up?' Kim shot back. 'Of course I'm talking about Steve. I've come here to ask you to think again. You're holding the threat of unemployment over his head like an axe, but you can't do this to him; he's an innocent man, he's done nothing wrong. You must realise you don't have a leg to stand on; you can't sack him—not without proof of misconduct. If you do that, you'll be taking a road which can only lead to trouble.'

She seated herself in the black leather chair that was in front of the desk, crossing her long, nylon-clad legs.

His eyes followed the movement. He said, 'It's good of you to tell me how to do my job, Miss Darby, but unnecessary. Bennett has been suspended; that's not quite the same thing.'

'There can't be any grounds for suspending Steve,' Kim persisted. 'He wasn't in charge of the site for the majority of the time. The man you should be gunning for is working abroad now. Why aren't you pursuing him?'

'Bennett held the reins for long enough to clash with a major client. I won't see this company brought down by bad publicity. Masters is threatening to withdraw his contract, and that's bad news for everyone concerned.'

'It's no reason for you to pick on an innocent man to take all the flak. What are you doing to track down the man who's really responsible?'

Coulter shrugged. 'There will be investigations—that goes without saying. But I believe we'll come up with the same answer. Bennett. I realise that's not what you want to hear, but that's the way it is, I'm afraid.'

'No, you're wrong. Steve would never allow himself to become involved in anything bad.' She drew the small notebook from her bag and thrust it towards him. 'Look; he kept a record of all that went on every day on site—it's almost like a diary. You can see from that that there was nothing untoward going on.'

He flicked through the pages, his expression closed, revealing nothing. At last he said, 'In itself, this means nothing. Certainly, it shows the extent of his workload and some of his dealings, but it's what isn't written down there that counts.' He tossed the book across the table.

Kim glared at him, incensed by his arrogant indifference. 'What you're really saying is that you've condemned him out of hand and you intend to get him out, any way you can. It's what I might have expected from a ruthless, power-hungry individual like you.'

'Have you finished?'

'No. Not by a long way. You're so convinced of Steve's guilt—just what form are these so-called investigations going to take? Are you expecting to come up with evidence of some kind?'

'It seems likely.'

'Only if you manufacture it to suit your needs,' she muttered.

He gave her a hard stare. 'Be very careful, won't you? I can understand your concern for a relative, but you should think seriously about what you're saying.'

Her lip jutted. 'What other conclusion can I draw from your actions? You've taken an innocent man and cut him down to his knees. Don't you have any conscience at all? How do you imagine he will get another job at his age if you let him go?'

Coulter seemed bored by the whole situation. 'That's Bennett's problem, not mine.'

'You don't care, do you?' Kim accused, watching him, her expression pained. Her mother had been right. People didn't matter to him at all. She said slowly, 'He was with the firm long before you came along. Doesn't his loyalty over all the past years count for anything?'

'Keeping the customer satisfied is what it's all about. If things go wrong, there has to be a reckoning.'

'If anything was wrong about that job, then it has to be down to you,' she retorted. 'Your only concern is your profit margin. Steve worked long hours for you, along with all the other men on that site. You've been pushing to get the job finished right from the start. It would grieve you to have to pay out more than the minimum on labour costs, wouldn't it? And the same applies to the materials. If Masters is dissatisfied, it's all down to you, but you're not going to pay the price, are you? Oh, no, you've chosen someone else to cover your guilt. You've made Steve your scapegoat to appease your client.'

Coulter stood up and walked slowly around the table towards her. He did not take his eyes off her, and Kim belatedly remembered the two hundred or so pounds of dangerous animal lurking beneath the outward trappings of civilised man. When he stopped in front of her, she braced herself to look up into his cold, hard eyes, and for a few heart-stopping minutes she wondered if he might be considering finishing off what he had started the other night. Her fingers stole to her throat in a protective gesture.

He did not miss the significance of her action. His mouth curled nastily. 'Afraid, Miss Darby? Maybe you should be. That pretty mouth is going to land you in a lot of trouble one of these days. I hope Bennett appreciates what you're doing for him? Or has he already promised you a reward?'

She stood up to lessen the advantage he had over her. 'That's typical, isn't it? It's exactly how you would think of it, wouldn't you? In terms of cost and payment.' His height still threatened, but her heels made up for some lost inches, and at least her eyes were on a level with his shirt collar. 'Do you think I can be frightened away by your aggressive tactics? I'm not scared of you,' she flared angrily. 'Do your worst. I'll get another job soon enough; I have contacts.'

He said slowly, 'You think that's my worst?' He closed the gap between them, his mouth twisting, and by a great effort of will she stood her ground.

'If—if you try to persecute my stepfather, you'll regret it,' she muttered.

'Is that so?' He studied her thoughtfully. 'Thanks for the warning. If I'm going to be dealing with a dangerous woman I shall obviously have to think out my tactics carefully.'

'You surprise me,' Kim grimaced. 'I thought your repertoire only consisted of brute force.' She passed a hand lightly over her shoulder as if to ease it.

His brows rose. 'Sore, is it?' He bared his teeth, white and very even. 'Surely you're not suggesting that I rub it better?'

She took a step backwards. 'Don't you come any nearer. It's a wonder you didn't dislocate it. You don't know your own strength.'

'Considering the way you tried to emasculate me, I'd say we were about even, wouldn't you?' he murmured silkily, and she glowered at him, unwilling colour flaring in her cheeks. He would bring that up, wouldn't he?

Through her teeth she said, 'Shall we get back to the point under discussion?'

'By all means. Was there another slander you wanted to add to the list?'

She ignored the sarcasm in his tone. 'You'd do well to remember that I'm not easily put off,' she warned. 'And I do have one or two influential contacts if you should decide to go ahead with your victimisation of my stepfather.'

His eyes narrowed. 'Are you threatening me?' he asked, his voice dangerously soft.

'Think of it any way you like. I won't have my——'

The ringing of the telephone cut off what she had been about to say. He lifted the receiver, speaking briskly into the mouthpiece.

'Coulter here.'

Kim watched him in silence, saw the way his mouth curved attractively as he listened, heard the gentling note as he answered, and decided in disgust that his caller must be a woman.

Peevishly, she waited for the conversation to end, but he seemed to be in no hurry. He flicked a glance in her direction, and her foot tapped on the carpeted floor with barely disguised impatience. He half sat, half leaned on the desk, the dark material of his trousers stretched tight against the hard muscles of his thighs, and Kim looked away. She did not want to stay and listen to his honeyed tones, to see the warm glint in his eyes.

This was a side of Greg Coulter she had not seen before, and it bothered her, though she could not have said why. She caught his gaze as it returned fleetingly to her once more, and her restiveness increased. Why was she still here? She had said her piece, and there was really no point in staying any longer to play cat-and-mouse games.

Turning on her heel, she started towards the door, but without warning his hand snaked out and caught her wrist, closing around it. He hauled her back towards him, his eyes admonishing her.

To his caller, he said, 'I'll pick you up at seven, Helen,' then he slowly replaced the receiver, and turned his attention back to Kim. His lips made a grim line, the charm which he had exuded towards the woman on the other end of the line no longer in evidence. Kim regarded him sourly, then turned her gaze pointedly in the direction of the fingers biting into her tender skin. He released her, a humourless smile on his mouth.

'I hope you weren't thinking of leaving just yet,' he gritted softly. 'There are still things we have to discuss.'

'I believe I've said all that I came to say,' she told him coolly.

He gave a brief nod. 'I'm glad to hear it, because I happen to have one or two things I'd like to say to you. I doubt you've considered the wisdom of your action in coming here this way and hurling accusations right, left and centre. Perhaps with your "influential contacts" you consider yourself invulnerable.' He walked around the large desk and picked up a folder, which he opened and laid out on the table. Seating himself in the black leather chair, facing her, he leaned back, relaxed, his hands steepled.

'I wonder if you've forgotten the contract that you signed?'

She regarded him steadily. 'I haven't forgotten, and I shan't let it stand in the way of my doing what I think is right. You don't frighten me. I expected that you would want to terminate it.'

'Did you?' He drew the opened folder towards him, and glanced idly through the contents. 'According to your personnel file, you're an intelligent young woman. You've worked hard to make your way in what is, essentially, a male profession. Are you sure you want to throw it all away?'

Kim's grey eyes flickered. He had not lost any time, had he? Immediately he had recognised her name, he must have determined on checking up on her. By now, he had probably registered every minute detail in that cold, electronic brain of his.

She said, 'I don't believe in compromising my principles.'

He looked at her thoughtfully. 'Even though you have yet to acquire final experience for qualification?'

Her shoulders lifted negligently. 'Yours is not the only firm employing architects, and I do have another offer open to me, with or without references.'

Coulter let the folder drop on to the table. 'Then it's unfortunate that you will not be able to take it up.' Leaning back in his chair, he studied her through narrowed eyes.

Kim said slowly, 'I don't think I quite follow your line of reasoning.'

'No,' he murmured, 'you wouldn't. For a bright girl it appears you can be incredibly foolish at times. If you check the small print, you'll find that the contract that you entered with this company is binding for six months, and I have no intention of releasing you from it.'

'Why not? Do you relish having the enemy in your camp?'

His mouth curved faintly. 'Let's just say I have plans for you, Miss Darby.'

'Really?' Her brows rose. 'Am I supposed to tremble at the knees?'

The blue eyes moved over her slowly. 'What an interesting thought. It's possible, I suppose.' He got to his feet. 'In the meantime, you could tell Bennett that enquiries are going ahead, and he will be kept informed of progress. Searching my house again would be a fruitless activity. I don't keep company papers there.'

'Aren't you forgetting,' she pointed out tightly, 'that I no longer have a key?'

His stare was cynical. 'I wouldn't count on that stopping you.'

Kim drew in her breath. 'Do you set out to be offensive, or does it come naturally?'

He gave a crooked smile. 'That will be something for you to discover, won't it, Miss Darby, over the next few months?'

CHAPTER THREE

SERIOUSLY out of breath after her race from the
car park and along the interminable corridors of
Coulter Construction, Kim flew into her office
and threw her coat over the back of her chair.
She was late. Worse still, the meeting would
already be in progress, and that meant she would
be the focus of all eyes as she walked in, because
everyone else would have arrived promptly. Greg
Coulter's departmental conferences always
started on time. Kim groaned inwardly. Much as
she might want to rock the boat, she didn't want
to be hauled over the coals for such a mundane
infringement, or have to make excuses in front
of the assembled company.

Rummaging in her desk, she pulled out a notepad and pencil, and made a dash for the door,
jerking it open. Her spiky heel snagged on the
carpet, and her foot rocked unsteadily on its
slender support. There was an ominous creak,
and she glanced downwards, cursing silently.
That was all she needed, right now—for her heel
to break. She could only hope that she hadn't
done any major damage. Shoes could be an expensive item to replace. Treading more gingerly,
she headed for the lift, and emerged, minutes

later, on to the corridor which led to Coulter's
inner sanctum.

Outside the conference-room, she paused, col-
lecting her wits. The hand that she raised to the
door was trembling, she realised, and she held it
still on the handle. What was the matter with her?
So, she was late. Was that any reason for her
breath to be coming in short gasps, and her heart
to be hammering like a piston? It had been a bad
morning, so far; nothing had gone right—and if
she didn't slow down things were going to get out
of hand. The last thing she wanted was for Greg
Coulter to see her in a flap.

There was also the possibility that, if she went
rushing in, her heel might snap off completely,
and then she would really feel foolish. She tilted
sideways to examine her shoe once more with a
critical eye. It didn't look too stable, but it was
still in one piece; that was the main thing. If she
was careful, with luck, it should hold out for a
while yet. A scratch marred the smooth black
leather, she noticed with a slight frown.

She was studying it doubtfully when the door
opened, causing her hand to slip, and she heard
Greg's deep drawl coming from the direction of
the table opposite.

'Ah, Miss Darby. How good of you to join us.
I was just about to send Mike to find you.'

Her wary glance took in the cool blue of his
stare, the hard, sardonic thrust of his jaw, then
shifted sideways to encounter the quizzical gaze

of Mike Jennings, who was holding open the door.

Greg said, 'If you've quite finished adjusting your nylons, perhaps we could get on with the meeting?'

Kim straightened, faint colour tinging her cheeks. Stiffly, she walked into the room, uncomfortably aware of the light ripple of amusement which passed among the small gathering of people seated around the dark mahogany table.

'I'm sorry to have kept you all waiting,' she told them with quiet dignity. 'I had a few problems this morning.'

It was an understatement. First there had been no electricity, which meant the radio alarm had not woken her, and then there was the additional hazard of negotiating the various rooms, all without benefit of light, or heat. Worst of all, though, was that she had set off for work without even the comfort of a cup of coffee.

'Apology accepted, Miss Darby. I trust your problem didn't have anything to do with frozen pipes?'

She caught the glimmer in the depths of his blue eyes, and gave him a tight smile. 'Nothing at all, but thank you for your concern.'

He said briskly, 'Well, now you are here, perhaps you would be good enough to bring us up to date on the Ashford development. I'm

taking it for granted, of course, that you've
managed to fit us into your heavy schedule?'

The cynicism that threaded his voice put her
teeth on edge. If she had taken her time over the
project assigned to her, he had only himself to
blame, she reflected bitterly. It went against the
grain, having to work for a man she disliked so
intensely. In the beginning, she had thought that
being employed by Coulter Construction would
be something to take pride in, but her illusions
had swiftly been shattered on that score. What
she still could not fathom, though, after all the
harsh words that had gone between them, was
exactly why he had refused to let her go. There
was, after all, little to be gained by keeping her
on, except for a deepening and persistent clash
of personalities.

All this, on an empty stomach. Gloomily, Kim
eyed the coffee-pot which occupied a shelf on a
side-wall, then dragged her attention back to
Greg. He was watching her, much in the way that
a wolf must watch its prey, she thought, and
wished that she did not feel quite so vulnerable.
Maybe if she'd had time to do more with her hair
than to pull a brush through its shining length
she'd have been a little more composed. Having
it flow free from its usual neatly pinned style
made her feel insecure, as though she had been
deprived of a vital piece of armour.

She took a seat at the table, laying her notepad
down on its smooth surface, and began in a cre-

ditably calm, unhurried manner to deliver her progress report. He listened without comment. If he did not like what he heard, he made no sign of it, other than a slight narrowing of his eyes. When she had finished, he turned his attention to Mike, who hastily delved into his briefcase and began to read from a sheaf of papers.

Kim sat back in her chair, viewing Greg contemplatively, twisting her pencil between her fingers. Why did he not free her from her contract? It was sheer pig-headedness on his part, she decided. What other explanation could there be, except that he wanted to impose his will, and show who was master? Her thoughts roamed as the meeting went on, and the various members of the department made their speeches. She knew what they would be saying; she had made it her business to find out how things operated in Coulter's world, and her own professional curiosity had demanded satisfaction.

Frowning slightly, she turned her attention to the man who ran things. He did not appreciate being thwarted, especially not by a woman. If she had learned one thing over the last few weeks, it was that he liked to have his own way. He always knew exactly what he wanted, and made sure that he got it, in double-quick time, or there was trouble. Well, she could give him plenty of that, she thought, smiling grimly. She sat up with a jerk, the pencil snapping under the pressure of her fingers into two jagged pieces that flew across the table with a clatter.

Silence fell on the room. Heads turned in her direction. Retrieving the splintered remains, she struggled to ignore the curious glances that came her way. It was not an easy thing to do.

Dave Prescott cleared his throat and finished outlining the alterations he had made to his section of the Ashford development.

'It looks as though everything is pretty much on schedule,' Greg said, when Dave sat down. 'There are no major hitches that I can see, except for Miss Darby's section.' He turned an assessing gaze on her. 'You understand, don't you, that we have certain deadlines to meet?'

She returned his stare with what she judged to be commendable equanimity in the circumstances. 'Of course. But you have to accept that the layout of the flats is much more involved than that of the shop units, and is bound to take up more time.'

His lashes flickered. 'In that case, I'll see to it that you are given more help.'

A faint line etched itself into Kim's brow. Whatever reaction she had been expecting, it was not this outward gesture of understanding. In one simple statement he had turned what could have become a heated confrontation into something completely different. He had made a decision that on the one hand seemed to point to her inadequacy and on the other would probably earn him the respect of his employees. Her eyes narrowed. He was clever, far more astute than she had given him credit for. She would have to be careful.

He leaned back in his chair. 'Thank you for your time, everyone. We'll meet again in a fortnight to review the situation.'

Dismissed, the men got to their feet, making for the door, a quiet hum of conversation breaking out. The meeting had gone on for longer than expected, and it was close to lunchtime. Briefly, Kim's glance swept the room, resting momentarily on the coffee-pot, and then swinging back towards Greg.

He dealt swiftly with the papers on the table, pushing them into a leather-bound folder before moving over to the window to peer out, one hand raised flatly against the white frame. The dark jacket of his suit hung open to reveal another of the finely striped shirts that he favoured. He was surveying his domain, Kim thought, taking pleasure in the neatly landscaped buildings that made up the formidable empire of Coulter Construction UK.

She pushed back her chair and stood up. Mike and Dave, along with several others, would most likely be heading for the local pub, where they could get a good, hot meal at a relatively cheap price. Sometimes Kim joined them, but she didn't plan on doing that today. She gathered up her belongings.

'Don't go yet, Miss Darby.' Greg's voice cut across her path, firm, incisive, making her step falter. 'I'd like a word, if you will.'

Her lashes lowered momentarily to hide the quick flicker of her grey eyes. So there was to be a reckoning, after all. He might have put on a show of team spirit for the benefit of his male colleagues, but her silent opposition rankled with him. Her mouth tilted. Good.

'What was it that you wanted to talk about?' She looked at him directly.

'I think you know that already. But perhaps we'll start with the problems that made you late.' His dark brows lifted in enquiry.

'My alarm didn't go off.'

There was no wavering in his steady regard. He merely waited, and she gave a reluctant grimace. He was obviously not deceived, and was not going to rise to the bait of her deliberately casual answer.

'No electricity,' she intoned laconically. 'I think there may be something wrong with the wiring. It's fairly ancient, so it's only to be expected, I suppose.'

'What are you going to do about it?'

'My landlord will get some sticking-plaster repairs made, I expect. I doubt whether he'll consider a complete re-wire, but I can always hope. There are a few other things he could have done at the same time, but we shall see. You don't have to worry, though, I won't be late again.'

His smile was almost pleasant. 'I never worry, Kim. If things aren't to my liking, I do something about it, as no doubt you'll find out for yourself before long.' He turned his gaze towards the window once more, to the vista of compact, aesthetically pleasing buildings, and it was Kim's turn to wait in silence. He said, 'This company has grown up over several decades. It's a thriving institution, and so far it hasn't been afflicted by the downturns that have caused some less fortunate businesses to come to grief. I intend that it will stay that way.'

The blue eyes returned to study her, and she said, a soft taunt in her voice, 'You think it's just possible I might lose you a contract or two, and that could land you with a little local difficulty?'

'Is that what you would like? Is that what the delaying tactics are all about—obstructing me?'

Kim gave a light shrug. 'Why should I concern myself with you at all? I have other, more important things to occupy my thoughts.'

'Like the effect your actions might have on your colleagues?'

The calmly posed question startled her. 'I've no idea what you mean,' she replied quickly, her grey glance flicking upwards.

'You're a liar, Kim,' he murmured. 'You're perfectly well aware what would happen if you carried your plan through to its ultimate goal. That's why you're only playing at it. I doubt you really want to see all Mike and Dave's hard work washed down the drain, not to mention all the other people involved. You might hate my guts, but you draw the line at seeing your friends' jobs laid on the line.'

Her breath caught in her chest. Like a well-trained hit man, he had managed to penetrate the one weak spot in her defences. 'That sounds like blackmail to me,' she muttered, her tone thick with accusation.

He gave a short, humourless laugh. 'Does it?' He regarded her thoughtfully. 'I imagine you think what you're doing is in no way connected with such sordid goings on.'

He shifted away from the window and started towards her, his tall frame in the well-cut dark suit outlined starkly against the pale cream of the walls. 'Did you honestly believe that I could be provoked by your petty resentment into making a decision that I might regret later?' He gave a mocking half-smile as he approached her. His walk was an easy, loose-limbed stride, his movements lithe and supple like those of an athlete. 'You don't know me very well, do you, Kim?' he said slowly, closing the distance between them. 'I really think we should do something to remedy that situation, don't you? After all, constant argument is a pretty fruitless activity, wouldn't you agree?'

His vivid blue gaze flashed over her. 'There are, as you pointed out, other, more important things to occupy our time. I'm quite sure that if we tried hard enough we could find a way to work this thing out.'

He was close to her now, so close that she could see the firm texture of his skin, smell the clean, fresh fragrance of his cologne. Her grey eyes skittered uneasily, encountering the strong brown column of his throat, a *frisson* of awareness flowing unbidden through her body. Alarmed, she took a step backwards.

'What's wrong, Kim?' His tone mocked her. 'Where are all the sharp remarks and tight answers now? Don't tell me that you've drawn in your claws?'

She realised then what she should have discovered long ago—that he actually enjoyed goading her. Perhaps he thought she was helpless, that there was no way she could win.

She studied him through her lashes. 'You'll take care not to overplay your hand, won't you?' she warned in a silky undertone. 'It wouldn't be beyond me to slap a harassment charge on you.'

He laughed, a genuinely amused sound. 'You're a cool lady, aren't you, Kim? It wouldn't do for me to underestimate you, would it?' He shook his head, his mouth curving in a way that was somehow dangerously attractive. 'But tell me, what was it that you had in mind? You don't seriously think that a discussion such as we've been having would constitute a case for a tribunal?'

Kim was not sure she liked the way his blue eyes sparked. He was too confident, far too sure of himself, and that knowledge was unsettling; it made her nervous.

'I mean it,' she persisted, faint urgency threading her words. 'You won't get away with intimidating me, however subtle the attempt. I'll see you finish up in court.'

He said musingly, 'Is that so? I think you're making a big mistake, Kim.' He paused. 'Still, if you're determined to go ahead with the accusation——' his voice dropped in a way that was infinitely disturbing '—the least I can do is to give you a frame to hang it on.'

Behind her, the table brushed her legs, blocking off a retreat. Her grey eyes widened, taking in the firm intent written in his strong, lean features. His hands closed on her arms, and she found herself being drawn towards him, the pressure of his fingers light, but at the same time insistent. She tried to pull away from him, and found, to her dismay, that she could not. The slow thud of her heartbeat sounded heavily in her ears, and heat began to curl through her limbs in a slow spiral.

He was in no hurry, and it seemed to Kim that everything had taken on a dreamlike quality, as if she was mesmerised by his actions. She caught the silky gleam of his hair as he bent his head towards her, then his mouth brushed hers in a caress that was both warm and coaxing. Her mind reeled with stunned reaction to the unexpectedly sweet sensuousness of that kiss, and to the un-accountable feeling of loss that besieged her when it was over.

She stared at him blindly for a few seconds until reality took over, and she wrenched herself away from him, dragging the back of her hand over her mouth as if to wipe away any remnant of his touch.

Shock lent a brittle edge to her words. 'I warned you,' she said with vehemence. 'You seem to think you're a law unto yourself, that no one can knock you from that stone pedestal; but you're wrong.' His smile infuriated her. 'You won't get away with this,' she gritted, 'I'll make sure of it.'

'Will you?' His eyes mocked her. 'How will you do that, Kim? Where are your witnesses?'

She glared at him. 'You think you're so clever, don't you?' she muttered thickly. 'You're a fiend; you think you can walk all over everyone.'

His mouth twisted. 'Aren't you being a trifle melodramatic? Anyone would think that you had never been kissed before. Where have you been all your life? In a cloister?'

'Mind your own business,' she told him, her voice strained. 'You had no right to do that.'

'You deserved it,' he said shortly. 'You were so intent on giving me trouble, I decided it was time you had a little yourself. Why do you im-agine I'm keeping you to your contract? So that

I can indulge in a little dalliance on the side whenever the fancy takes me?'

Her mouth was set in a resentful line, and he studied her with impatience. 'Take my word for it,' he said coldly, 'you're quite safe. I have neither the time nor the inclination to initiate a prim little virgin into the joy of sex.'

Kim stiffened, feeling her cheeks begin a slow burn. The almost imperceptible flick of her head sent a shimmer of light quivering through the thick mass of her hair. 'I'm glad you feel that way,' she said slowly, through her teeth, 'because, believe me, you wouldn't get the chance. And now——' she glanced down at her watch '—I have to go.' She moved her lips in a tight smile. 'A lunch-date,' she said. 'If you'll excuse me?'

He replied, the ghost of amusement in his eyes, 'That stung, did it, Miss Prim? Be in my office at one-thirty, won't you? There are things we need to discuss—among them, your role in this department.'

She cast an icy stare in his direction and stalked past him, out of the room, furiously aware of the soft laughter on his breath as she went.

No one, she fumed, had ever had the power to annoy her as much as this man. Why did she let him get to her this way? If it weren't for his threat that he would make life distinctly uncomfortable for her if she left the company, she would have walked out there and then. But she did not know what form his retaliation would take, and she dared not risk it. Knowing Greg, even for a short time, was enough to make her think twice now about any action she took. There was always the awful possibility that he would exact revenge on Steve as well as herself, and she did not want that on her conscience. Steve had enough troubles.

Richard Villiers was already seated at a discreet corner table in the small, neat restaurant, which was just a short walk from the office, when Kim arrived a while later. The fresh air had gone some way towards calming her, so that when she greeted him her manner was reasonably relaxed. Why should she allow Greg Coulter to spoil her lunch?

'I hope I'm not too late,' she said. 'The meeting went on a bit.'

Richard got to his feet, a smile creasing his handsome face as he leaned over to kiss her lightly on the cheek. 'Not at all,' he murmured. 'I've only been here a minute or two myself.'

They sat down, and a waiter came over to hand them each a menu. Kim studied hers briefly. The decision was an easy one to make. She would have a salad. She always preferred something light at this time of day.

'I remember Coulter's meetings always lasted around a couple of hours,' Richard said when their orders had been taken. 'He would make a point of covering every aspect, making sure nothing had been missed. Eyes like a hawk, that man.' There was a touch of rancour in the words, and Kim gave him a thoughtful, frowning look.

'I'd forgotten that you once worked for him,' she said. 'That must have been some time ago—you've been in business for yourself for a few years now, haven't you?'

'Four years this month,' Richard agreed. 'It's a move that was long overdue.'

'So things are going well?' Kim queried lightly, shaking out her napkin as the meals arrived. 'I heard that you were looking at various projects in Scandinavia.'

Richard paused, spearing succulent flakes of fish delicately with his fork before answering. 'That's true. If I landed one of those, I'd be all right.' He ate slowly for a moment or two, then said, 'The competition's pretty stiff, you know. It's heartbreaking in a way. We're constantly coming up with sound, imaginative ideas, yet we still lose contracts that should be ours—mostly to Coulter. I'd give anything to throw a spanner in his works.'

Kim ran a careful finger around her wine glass, worried by the tang of bitterness that flavoured his words. 'Is it that bad?'

His lips parted a fraction, as if he was about to say something, but then changed his mind. He shook his head. 'We're doing all right. Mostly we get the smaller contracts, the stuff that Coulter isn't interested in. Sooner or later, I'll find out how he's getting the better of me. Then we'll see who wins in a fair fight.' He hesitated, giving her a searching glance. 'How are things with you? Perhaps I shouldn't be saying these things to you, as you're part of his team now. Are you settled with the company?'

Kim pulled a face. 'Let's just say that I'm making the best of it.'

Richard put down his fork. 'You could always come and work for me.' He took a swallow from his ice-cold lager, and waited for her answer.

'I wish it were that easy,' Kim said quietly. 'It's what I'd like to do, but I signed a contract, and there's no way I can get out of it. Whatever we might think of him, Greg Coulter has a lot of influence in some circles.'

'You mean that if you eventually wanted to go it alone he could put the word about and stop you from getting work? Unreliability, temperament, and that sort of thing?'

She bit her lip. 'I suppose so.'

Richard muttered something under his breath. 'There has to be a way of putting a stop to him. One day I'll find it.'

The waiter appeared to refill Kim's glass with wine, and to offer the sweet-trolley. When they had made their selection and ordered coffee, Richard leaned back in his chair, viewing Kim with affection. 'Don't let Coulter grind you down. I'll always be here, waiting. If things get too much, come to me. We'll sort something out.'

It was just before one-thirty when Kim walked into Greg's outer office. This time his secretary made no attempt to stop her—was not, in fact, anywhere to be seen.

'And how did your lunch-date go?' There was the faintest emphasis on the word 'date'. Greg appeared in the doorway, his tall figure leaning casually against the door-jamb, the wicked hint of a grin lurking about his mouth. He had discarded his jacket, and the cuffs of his shirt were drawn back to reveal strong, sinewy forearms, dark hair contrasting with the tanned skin. It was no wonder he induced a kind of breathless hysteria in the women members of his staff, Kim reflected sourly. Looks like his ought to be banned as seriously damaging to female emotional stability.

She flicked him a contemptuous glance, and the grin widened, his teeth showing white and even.

'Come through,' he said, going through to his own room. 'Do you want a coffee? Grab yourself a cup from the cupboard over there.'

Kim stared after him in confusion. He was a man of great contrasts, and she was not entirely sure that she knew how to deal with his changes of mood. She had thought that as long as she kept her wits about her she could just about cope with the hard-headed businessman, but this good-humoured stranger was another matter entirely.

'What are you waiting for? Cups are on the shelf, spoons in the drawer. If you don't want one, I certainly do.' He fiddled with the lid of the percolator, and flicked his gaze back to her unmoving figure.

Kim took a swift hold on herself, and did as he asked. He poured, and pushed a cup of the hot liquid towards her. He said briskly, 'If you and I are to have any kind of working relationship——' her mouth opened, and he went on drily '—and I mean that we shall, then certain differences will have to be aired.'

'Like why you insist on treating Steve as though he were a criminal?' she put in swiftly. 'I'll agree to that. Why are you hounding him?'

'You're the one who keeps putting it into such strong terms,' he admonished her coolly. 'For myself, I prefer to reserve judgement until I have proof of what has been going on.'

'I assume you're looking for something in particular?' she persisted.

He shrugged. 'I've come up against all sorts of things in this business—deals on the side, backhanders for pushing certain products, doctoring the accounts——'

'Steve wouldn't do anything like that——'

'Maybe not.'

He sounded indifferent, and Kim's temper flared. 'He would not. You've known him for years; you must know what kind of man he is.'

'I thought I did.'

There wasn't a scrap of emotion in the way he said it, and she glowered at him angrily. 'You've tossed this idea into the pot out of the blue because you know Masters wants heads to roll and you're making certain it isn't going to be yours on the block.'

He considered her thoughtfully. 'Heads will roll,' he said. 'It could be that, as you suggested, the foreman on site was responsible. He's somewhere in Asia at the moment, but no doubt we'll track him down eventually. Then again, Steve appears to be the most likely candidate, possibly aided and abetted by his stepdaughter. It does seem rather odd that you are so vigorously active in his defence and in the undermining of my company from the inside.'

'Definitely a case for bringing in the tanks, then,' she retorted. 'Is it really possible that such a minor cog can cause such a lot of damage?' She smiled and gave a tremulous sigh, as though the thought gave her a sweet thrill of pleasure.

He gave a soft, disconcerting chuckle. 'Hardly so dangerous,' he murmured, 'that I couldn't deal with the matter personally—hand to hand, so to speak.'

Kim was not sure what she read in the depths of his blue eyes, but whatever it was it worried her. So did the slight upward tilt that came to his mouth as he watched her indecision, and the seemingly relaxed attitude of his long, lithe body only an arm's length away.

'In fact——' He stirred, and she was immediately aware that the indolent manner served only to cloak his powerful male vitality. Her throat was suddenly very dry. Twisting around, she had no thought in her head but to run, to make for the door, and safety.

It was that—the reckless speed of her movements—that was her undoing. She heard the wrench at the same time that her heel turned and wavered, and the support slid away from under her foot. Desperately trying to regain her balance, she bit back a cry of pain and clung on to the nearest solid object available, using it as a lever to get herself upright once more.

'Are you all right?' Concern sounded in his voice.

'I th—my shoe—oh!' Her fingers gripped the hard-muscled warmth of his shoulder, and she stared at them in dismay, as if they could not possibly belong to her. 'I'm sorry; I didn't mean to...' She removed them with a jerk, and found herself swaying again, one foot adrift on a choppy sea.

A strong arm locked around her waist, steadying her. 'I've got you,' Greg said. 'Keep hold, this time, and let's see what the problem is.' He knelt down beside her, his hand moving to rest lightly on her leg, and a shuddery heat ran, unbidden, through her veins. The slow, smooth glide of his fingers over her calf and down towards her ankle sent her temperature soaring way out of bounds, and she gave a small squeak of protest. She tried to hop away, and his arm tightened on her.

'Stop squawking like an overheated schoolgirl and for goodness' sake stand still.' He inspected her ankle, feeling with careful thoroughness all around, and said, 'I don't think you've done any major damage. It'll probably be sore for a while, though.' He retrieved her errant shoe, and looked up at her, the devilish quirk to his mouth back in evidence. 'Serves you right for letting your imagination get the better of you.'

She chose to ignore his remark, turning her head away in what she hoped was a dignified silence as he stood up. When he had helped her over to a chair, he picked up the dislodged heel and proceeded to hammer it home with a heavy paperweight.

'That should see you through the rest of the day,' he told her, handing it back to her a few minutes later. 'Provided, of course, that you don't make any more hasty moves.'

Her face set in mutinous lines, and he continued bluntly, 'Let's get something straight, shall we? You were set on in this company because I wanted a woman architect as part of my team, and that remains the case today. I want a balance of viewpoints. Your qualifications are good—the best—and you have vision, if only you will keep

your mind running along the right track. All you
need is experience, and you can get that here,
with this firm.'

He put the paperweight on the table, and went
on roughly, 'Your stepfather's argument with me
doesn't come into it, and you'll be doing yourself
a disservice if you let it get in the way of your
career. No matter what contacts you have, a year
or two with this company will be a considerable
advantage when you finally come up against the
outside market.'

Kim swallowed uncomfortably, still uncertain.
'So far,' she said haltingly, 'my viewpoint hasn't
been of particular importance.'

'It will be.' He considered her shrewdly,
gauging her response. 'This weekend, for instance. I want you to come with me to
Derbyshire.'

CHAPTER FOUR

KIM sat up very straight in her chair and stared at Greg through narrowed eyes. 'Derbyshire?' she repeated, slowly.

He nodded. 'I've a meeting with the local planning officer late on Friday afternoon, and afterwards a dinner appointment. I thought we'd drive over at lunchtime. Then, on Saturday, I want to take a look at a site over there. I'll need you to go over it with me, see what ideas we can come up with between us.' He saw her hesitation and frowned questioningly. 'Is there some problem?'

She cleared her throat. 'I've already made arrangements for this weekend,' she said.

'Break them. This is more important.'

Her brows rose in a delicate arch. 'To you, perhaps.'

He regarded her thoughtfully. 'Do I have to remind you of your contract? There is a clause about occasional weekend working.'

'That may be so,' Kim replied coolly, 'but surely I am entitled to rather more than one day's notice?'

'What plans have you made?' He threw the question at her, and Kim viewed him cautiously.

'I've accepted invitations for Friday and Saturday evening,' she said.

He inclined his head slightly in acknowledgement. 'Would you consider driving over on Saturday morning if I give you directions? After we're through, I've to see one of the local councillors, so you'll be free to return home by midafternoon—that should give you plenty of time to socialise, shouldn't it?'

'I—suppose so,' Kim murmured. He had offered a compromise solution, and it was hardly possible to refuse.

He gave her a wolfish smile. 'Don't sound too enthusiastic, will you?'

The matter was settled. Turning away, Greg tore a sheet of white paper from a pad and started to sketch out a rough drawing, adding beneath it some brief notes. He handed it to her and she gave it a cursory glance.

'You should have no difficulty in finding it.' His tone was cool and brisk. 'We'll meet at the site. Two o'clock. Don't be late.'

Saturday was a raw, cold day that had degenerated steadily into wintry storms. The temperature had dropped to a biting degree, and Kim had discovered to her cost that some of the sideroads were dangerous with ice. Shakily, she stood and rubbed at her shoulder where the seatbelt had cut in, and surveyed the buckled wing of her car with growing despondency.

Why did things have to happen in this aggravating way? Just when she most needed the money, she was saddled with two bills—one for shoes and the other for car repairs. At this rate her savings would never amount to anything. She sighed deeply and turned up the collar of her coat, pulling the lapels close around her to keep in what warmth she could. Already the sky was darkening, and her mood, as she trudged towards the bluff where Greg stood waiting, matched the bleakness of the wind-swept landscape.

He had been looking out over the tree-lined valley below, but, as she made her way carefully over the craggy ground, her legs still weak in the aftermath of shock from her accident, he glanced irritably at his watch and demanded, 'Where on earth have you been? I've been standing here for half an hour.'

Kim bit back a sharp retort. There was no telling how he would react to her explanation, but she didn't feel up to an inquisition and caustic comments about women drivers. Her head ached intolerably from its earlier collision with the headrest, and she just wanted to get the afternoon over with. She still had to find a garage that would send someone along to look at her car. With her luck, they'd all have shut up shop and gone home by the time she had finished work. Head lowered, she searched in her bag for a notepad, and mumbled her excuses into the fleece lining of her jacket. He said, in a voice shot through with impatience, 'Well, now you are here, let's get on with it.'

He strode away briskly, leaving Kim to struggle as best she could to keep up with him as he took a route that circled the valley. As he went, he outlined the various features that he wanted incorporated into the final plans for the business park which was to be his latest project. It was to blend in with the scenery, not detract from it in any way. Kim listened, and made notes with fingers that still trembled from the day's earlier events, the wind whipping at her paper.

The afternoon wore on. Whenever she caught her mind drifting to the débâcle with the car, she pulled it sharply into line. Greg moved on, tirelessly, his long legs covering the slippery, grassy slopes with ease. Kim followed, viewing his energetic figure with vague feelings of irritation. Every now and again she paused to take photographs of the valley, adjusting the camera with cold fingers to get the best results. Back in the office her first job would be to reflect on the site from all its different angles so that she was fully aware of all the possibilities.

'That'll do for today,' Greg announced at last, and Kim stifled a sigh of relief, turning her head away from the wind to push back the wispy tendrils of hair that had blown across her face. Sleet had begun to swirl about them, leaving fat droplets of cold moisture to soak into her coat.

'We'd better get out of this before it gets any worse,' Greg said, looking at the ominously grey sky. Kim nodded heartfelt agreement and pushed her notepad into her bag, slinging the camera over her uninjured shoulder. They started back towards the road, and he asked, 'Where did you leave your car? I don't see it anywhere.'

She swallowed against the lump in her throat. 'It's...off the main road,' she answered, her voice low and slightly uneven. Greg's sleek-bodied Aston Martin waited over the next rise, and, as they approached it, she said quietly, 'Well, I expect I shall see you in the office on Monday.' She began to walk away.

'Wait,' he said. 'I'll give you a lift to your car.'

'No,' she replied quickly, too quickly, because his head lifted and he eyed her pale face narrowly. 'There's really no need,' she added in a more controlled manner. 'It isn't far, and I prefer to walk.'

She started to back away, a harried look creeping into her grey eyes, and he watched her, his expression quizzical. 'I insist,' he murmured. 'Your face is ghostly white, you look as if you're halfway to a block of ice, and I'd hate you to catch a chill and blame it on to me. With victimisation and harassment charges already laid at my door, I consider I've quite enough to contend with.' He opened the passenger door of his car. 'Which way do we head?' he asked.

Kim hesitated in the face of determined opposition. 'I—uh——' She gritted her teeth. 'The nearest garage would be a good idea,' she pronounced at last. Just let him say one word, that's all, just one.

'I see.' He paused, considering her. 'And might I ask what the problem is? Lack of petrol? Or worse?'

Her lower lip jutted. 'I am perfectly capable of keeping my tank topped up,' she informed him tightly. 'I skidded on a patch of ice, trying to avoid some madman who took a bend too wide, and consequently my car is out of action—at least, until I can get it off the slab of stone that someone left on the verge.'

He frowned. 'It wouldn't have occurred to you to tell me about this before, I suppose?'

'When? After you bawled me out for being late? I'd hardly be fool enough to invite a lecture on my driving ability as well, would I?'

A muscle clenched in his jaw. Opening the door wider, he pushed her down into the vehicle with the aid of a firmly directed palm on her head. 'Get in,' he said tersely. 'You'd better show me the damage.'

Once she had given him directions, she maintained a gloomy silence in the depths of the luxurious car. The smell of the plush leather upholstery and the cushioning warmth of her seat were only a borrowed comfort. She could not give in to the urge to rest her aching head against the padded support and allow her weary body to relax. She had things to sort out, and she needed all her faculties about her.

By now the sleet had turned to snow, heavy flakes that were beginning to settle on the hedge-rows and weigh down the branches of trees that overhung the road. The car ran smoothly over the wet surface, purring along, with Greg maintaining a light, easy control on the steering. Kim risked a troubled sideways glance at his hard profile. The flint-like expression did nothing to ease her tension; he was scowling darkly, his mouth firmed into a tight line. He had said something about a meeting after the day's work was finished, and she was unhappily aware that she was keeping him from it.

They found her Mini as she had left it, slewed to a halt at a reckless angle on the grass verge, the wing buckled where it had caught the nearby tree in a side-swipe. Greg's breath hissed sharply between his teeth as he climbed out of the car to take a look. She followed him, standing silent and morose as the snow fell about her with chilling, damp persistence. He went around to the front of the car, and bent down to inspect the chassis.

'Sit behind the wheel,' he said curtly, 'and release the handbrake when I tell you.'

She did as she was told, heart in her mouth as he put his shoulder to the bonnet and shoved with all his strength. The car rocked on the boulder and then grudgingly began to inch backwards, and she turned the wheel to bring it back into line. Greg straightened, drawing air deeply into his lungs a few times before coming around to the side-window.

She wound it down. 'Thanks,' she said gratefully. 'Is it all right to start up the engine now?'

His stare was incredulous. 'You surely don't think you're going anywhere in that wreck?' He took a clean handkerchief from the pocket of his suede coat and grimly proceeded to wipe the dirt from his hands. She noticed with a pang of guilt that his jacket was stained where he had applied it to the front of her car.

'I—I just thought,' she stammered, 'that with a bit of luck it might hold together enough to get me home.'

'Take my advice,' he gritted. 'Don't think, not unless you can come up with something better than that. You've a crack in your sump and you're losing oil. Even casting aside any other damage there might be, you're not likely to get more than half a mile.'

'Oh.'

'Oh, indeed.' Greg's tone reflected the granite set of his features. 'I don't imagine there's any chance that you belong to a motoring organisation?'

Kim's mouth opened and then closed again. She shook her head. 'I was going to get around to it some time.'

He gave her a wintry smile. 'I thought as much,' he said. 'You really oughtn't to be allowed out on your own.' His cool blue eyes appraised her slowly, and Kim was drearily conscious of her cold nose and the way her hair clung wetly to her face, little rivulets of water running down to the well of her collar.

'Go back to my car,' he rasped. 'I'll sort something out.'

His annoyance was understandable, she supposed, but she didn't feel much like apologising. If the man had even an ounce of humanity he would know that she'd had enough for one day and could do without his censorious manner. It was all his fault she was here anyway.

He used his car-phone to call up a breakdown service, then jabbed in another set of numbers to put him in touch with the councillor he was to have met. Losing interest in the ensuing conversation, Kim shifted her bruised shoulder carefully against the back of her seat, easing it a little. She closed her eyes fleetingly against the throbbing pain that had lodged resolutely inside her head.

The man from the garage was not optimistic about the fate of her crumpled blue Mini. 'It'll be a couple of weeks, I should think, if not more, before she's back on the road,' he commented after he had taken a quick survey. 'Spare parts could take a while, and that wing's not going to be a five-minute job.'

Kim groaned, and Greg handed the man a business card, with a murmured, 'See if you can hurry things up, will you? There could be a bonus in it for you. Give me a ring when it's road-worthy again.'

The man's gaze flickered from Greg to the Aston Martin and back again, and he nodded. 'I'll see what I can do,' he agreed.

As they drove away, Kim said with an in-flexion of disapproval, 'Did I just witness bribery and corruption in action?'

'Stop complaining,' Greg returned hardily, 'or I'll dump you in the middle of the road, here and now.'

He did not sound as if he was joking, and Kim snapped her lips shut. She let her head sink back on to the head-rest, and felt her eyelids droop. The smooth motion of the car had a soothing effect on her rattled nerves; her mind drifted like the snow that fell in a white blanket around them, and her last conscious thought was one of relief that finally they were headed for home.

When she awoke, music from a local radio station was filtering quietly through the stereo system. She looked around, dazedly for a moment, then glanced out of the window, blinking in confusion to discover that, instead of being on the motorway as she had expected, they were turning into the drive of a sturdy stone-built cottage.

'Where are we?' she asked in a puzzled, sleep-husky voice, tiredly stretching her limbs and feeling once more the dampness of her coat seep through to chill her body. 'Why aren't we on the motorway?'

'Haven't you noticed what's happened to the weather?' Greg replied. 'I'm not going any further in these conditions. We'll stay here until it clears.'

'But——' she sat up stiffly and peered at the house '—what is this place? It doesn't look like a hotel, or a guest-house. We can't just barge in on people unannounced.'

'We won't be doing that.' He switched off the ignition. 'The house is empty. It belongs to me—we'll be all right here for the weekend. I use it quite often when I want a break, so I make sure there are always some supplies in.'

Kim said very slowly, 'I can't stay here. I have to go home.'

'Forget that idea for tonight,' he told her brusquely. 'Take a look around. Only someone completely off their head would attempt to drive any distance in that.' He looked at her as if that was exactly the sort of thing he would have expected her to do.

'I'll get a train,' she decided. 'Is there a phone in the house? I'll find out the time of the next one.'

'What's the rush?' he asked impatiently. 'You'd still have to battle your way to the station, and nothing can be so urgent that you have to race home tonight.'

'Even so,' she said firmly, 'I want to try.'

He smiled briefly, without humour. His long fingers flicked the window at his side. 'See that out there? That's what we call a blizzard.' His tone was ultra-patient, as if he were dealing with a recalcitrant child. 'According to the latest news bulletin, conditions further north are much worse than this, and the trains are running either extremely haphazardly or not at all.'

Kim chewed uneasily at her lip. 'There must be some way I——'

'No,' he interrupted harshly, 'there isn't, or I'd have found it by now. We're staying here, and that's the end of it. If the thought of spending the night with me worries you, that's just too bad.'

Heat filled Kim's cheeks. 'I wasn't——'

'Yes, you were.' His blue eyes were scathing. 'But, I'm telling you, I'm not risking life and limb just to soothe your neurotic temperament. It's all your fault that we have to stay over, anyway. If you hadn't wound yourself round a tree, and we hadn't been obliged to stay and sort it out, we might just have reached home before the worst of the weather came. But we didn't, so now you can do yourself a favour and get out of the car and into the house before I lose my temper completely.' He swung out of the driver's seat and slammed the door shut with a violence that sent shock waves reverberating through the car.

Kim followed him to the door of the cottage. 'I don't know why you're so angry,' she began tautly. He glowered as he thrust a key into the lock. 'I didn't ask to come here,' she went on, 'and I am at least trying to get out of your way.' She shivered in the cold air, her breath freezing into fine mist. 'I'd absolutely hate to be any trouble to you.'

His mouth made a sardonic curve. 'Lady, you can't help it. Trouble follows you around.' The door swung open, and he pushed his way into the house.

Kim stood and glared at his wide shoulders for a long moment, then went after him into the large, well-lit hall. The walls were textured, and hung with pleasing landscape paintings. A finely worked oval rug lay at her feet, covering highly polished wood blocks.

Greg walked through to the sitting-room, where he knelt down to set a match to the fire already laid in the grate. 'It'll take a while to warm up.' He got to his feet, giving her jacket a disparaging glance. 'You had better take that off,' he said tersely. 'I should think it's soaked right through. I'll see if I can find you a sweater to wear.'

He waited while she slid the coat awkwardly from her complaining shoulders, then he took it and disappeared upstairs. Kim stared down at the orange and yellow flames crackling in the hearth, and rubbed at her arms absently, feeling cold, and strangely forlorn. Pain throbbed at her temples.

'Here; put this on.' She jumped as Greg's deep voice sounded in her ear. 'It'll be too big, but that won't matter.'

'Thank you,' she said stiffly. She heard the brittleness of her tone, and saw the derision that immediately darkened Greg's eyes. The sweater was beige wool, thick and warm-looking, and he watched as Kim lifted her arms to pull it on over her own thinner top, his gaze travelling with mocking contempt over her slender curves.

Her mouth tightened. He was doing it to provoke her. Well, two could play at that game. She returned his stare, letting her grey eyes wander with lazy insolence from his hard-boned features to the black sweatshirt that hugged his broad chest, and down over the denim jeans that fit snugly over his lean hips and powerful thighs. It was not a wise move. Her throat felt suddenly very dry, and her glance skittered away. He was too intensely masculine, much too overwhelmingly vital for the intimate surroundings of this small cottage. She felt ill just thinking about being here alone with him, miles from anywhere.

'Satisfied?' he queried, amusement threading his voice.

'I'm sure it will be a great help,' she said coolly, deliberately misunderstanding him.

His mouth made a wicked curve. 'Anything to be of service,' he murmured silkily. 'I'd have suggested brandy might be just the thing to— thaw you out, but perhaps coffee would be safer in the circumstances.'

She drew in a sharp, deep breath, and he laughed outright, turning to walk from the room. Damn the man, she thought wretchedly; why could she not learn to ignore his baiting? His greatest pleasure was to wind her up.

After a minute or two she took a hold on herself and went and sat down on a chair facing the hearth. It was the torments she had undergone throughout this ill-fated weekend that made her feel so weak at the knees, she told herself. It was nothing to do with Greg Coulter and the insidious threat he posed.

He came back a short while later bearing a tray laden with cups and a coffee-pot. There was a plate of sandwiches too, and she looked at him in surprise.

'Freezer and microwave,' he explained, reading her mind. 'Amazing modern contraptions. Help yourself. I couldn't be bothered with anything more elaborate this evening.' He sat down, yawning, and stretched his long limbs.

Kim poured the coffees, and pushed a cup across the table towards him. 'You mentioned that you used the house a lot,' she said into the silence. 'Presumably you meant weekends? Do you have family living close by?'

He added cream to his cup. 'My brother and his wife. But more often than not I come here to be alone. I like to walk, and enjoy the country air.'

'I had noticed,' she muttered, registering the unaccustomed stiffness of her calf muscles.

'I hope you're not expecting sympathy,' he retorted, giving her legs a quick once-over. 'It's your fault entirely if you walked the couple of miles or so from your car to the site and then went round for two more hours without saying a word. If you will insist on being so rigidly independent, you've only yourself to blame when things go wrong. You ought to try out a few normal human emotions once in a while. It could do wonders for your system.'

His cold reaction was too much, coming on top of all that had happened. Kim's body recoiled as if from a blow, and her mouth wavered slightly. She clamped it, taking a breath until she had regained control. Coldly, she said, 'What would a walking automaton like you know about emotions? You don't have any deep feelings—that's why it's so easy for you to get rid of people around you, people who have been loyal to you and your company for more years than you can remember.' She picked up her coffee-cup, nestling it in both hands, and frowned moodily at the fire over the rim.

Greg took a small bottle from the tray and shook two white tablets out into his palm, holding them out to her.

'Aspirin,' he volunteered. 'You look as if you need them.' She stared at him, open-mouthed. 'They might do something to improve your disposition, too,' he added laconically.

She took the pills from him, and said, stone-faced, 'My disposition would be a lot sweeter if I did not have to listen to your constant criticism.'

He gave her a smile that bore no relation to the real thing. 'Dealing with a mule-head brings out the worst in me. Still, I dare say you might feel better if you soaked in the bath for a while and then followed it up with a good night's sleep. The guest bedroom's on the opposite side to the bathroom.' He leaned back in his chair, linking his hands behind his head. 'The water should be hot enough by now, if you want to try it. You'll probably find a clean robe in the cupboard.'

'I—thank you,' she said uncertainly, thrown off balance by his apparent mood change. 'I'd like that.'

She started to gather up the crockery from the table, but he stopped her, saying, 'Leave those; I'll stack them in the dishwasher later.' He yawned again, and she paused, then picked up her bag and went to the door.

As she reached it, he murmured, 'Oh, by the way, the lock on the bathroom door is faulty, but don't let that worry you. I promise I'll do my very best to curb my animal instincts.'

His soft laughter followed her as she mounted the stairs, and she gritted her teeth. 'I hate you, Greg Coulter,' she muttered under her breath. 'I really, really hate you.'

She could not be sure that he would not torment her just for the sake of it, so, as a precaution, she rammed a chair beneath the handle of the door before climbing into the tub of hot water. Soaking, as he had suggested, did help ease some of the aches caused by her collision with the tree. The bruising on her shoulder stretched diagonally, in line with the angle of the seatbelt, red and angry-looking, but there were no other visible marks. She washed her hair gingerly, taking care over the tender area at the back of her head.

Slipping a robe over her underwear, she went into the guest-room and dried her hair, then brushed it until it fell in softly gleaming waves to her shoulders.

When she had finished, she lay down on the bed, and drew the quilt around her with a faint sigh. Sleep would come as a welcome relief from the relentless buzzing in her head.

It must have been some three or four hours later when she stirred restlessly from a troubled slumber to realise that the little hammers inside her skull were not going to allow her any respite. Aspirin, she thought wearily. There must be some in the bathroom cabinet. The ones that Greg had given her hadn't had much effect, but another couple might help. She looked about her for a while, adjusting herself to the darkness of the room and the unfamiliar shadows before sliding out of bed and reaching for her borrowed robe.

A muted lamp glowed in the passageway, and she stood for a moment, uncertain which way to turn. It all looked strange in the dim light, and she was oddly disorientated. Hesitantly, she fumbled her way towards the bathroom, until her fingers tangled with the door-knob and she quietly pushed her way in, searching for the pull-cord. A golden glow suddenly filled the room, making her blink. Her hand was still intent on finding the switch.

Greg shifted his weight on the wide bed so that he was half turned towards her, leaning on one elbow, his bare shoulder propped up against the pillows. His brilliant blue gaze travelled lazily over the length of her, from the tousled mane of her hair, over the softly clinging robe, and down along the smooth line of her legs, before he brought it back up to rest on her stunned face. His smile was slow, curious. Husky-voiced, he murmured, 'Is anything wrong?'

Soundlessly, Kim shook her head. Swallowing against the constriction of her throat, she dazedly willed her wavering hand to leave its fruitless search and drag together the loose edges of her robe.

Greg said softly, 'Am I to take it that you decided on the brandy, after all?' Still she did not answer, and after a momentary pause he began to push back the bedcovers, allowing her a glimpse of tanned, bare skin. With the movement, Kim's numbed brain clicked into instant sharp focus, and she gave a faint yelp of alarm, stumbling backwards out of the door and tugging it firmly shut behind her.

Breathing erratically, she made off in the opposite direction and, at last, with a small exclamation of relief, discovered the whereabouts of the bathroom. The cabinet, though, did not yield any pain-killers, and she rested her hot brow against the cool glass while she collected her thoughts. Downstairs...on the table; that was where they would be. He obviously hadn't bothered to put them away.

She retraced her steps to the sitting-room, feeling her toes curl into the wool pile of the carpet. She stood for a moment and gazed into the dying embers of the fire. Looking around, she noticed that the pill bottle was on the tray where Greg had left it, and she picked it up, pushing her thumb against the plastic top to lever it off. It did not budge, and she tried again. Still nothing. She pressed her lips together in a grimace of disgust and frustration, and tormented the lid, pressing harder, until, with a sharp plop of release, the top shot off and little white tablets scattered in a confetti-like shower all over the floor. Kim ran a distracted hand through her hair. Cursing vehemently under her breath, she got down on her hands and knees to retrieve the wayward pills from their hiding place under the table.

Behind her, Greg tutted softly. 'That's hardly very ladylike, now, is it?' She turned her head swiftly at the intrusion, and he said, 'The language, I mean. The pose is fine.'

She stared at him blankly, and he added in a low drawl, 'Very sexy. For a beginner, you're learning fast.'

Kim jerked so rapidly that she banged her head on the table-top, and let out a small, aggravated squeal. A vase wobbled precariously and fell to the floor, shattering into a dozen or more jagged pieces. She scrambled out from her cramped position, and sat cross-legged on the carpet, clutching her head, and wailed, careless of the debris all around her.

Greg's arm thrust forward, his palm open in peremptory demand. 'Here, take my arm—get up out of there.' She slapped it away. Amusement glittered in his eyes, and that set the spark to her temper, shooting it skywards like a wayward rocket.

'Don't you laugh at me, you monster.' She rained a series of blows on the hands that were still trying to lift her from the floor, and when his lips twitched it was altogether too much; her mind hazed over in a red fury, and she balled her hand into a fist and smacked him hard in the mouth.

'Ouch!' He put the back of his hand to the place where a trickle of blood had begun to seep slowly. 'That hurt,' he muttered, wiping it away.

'Good,' she said on a choked sob. 'I'm glad.' Her arms flailed as he moved. 'Don't you touch me. Don't you come near me or I'll do it again. I hate you, Greg Coulter. I hate you and your rotten company, and your rotten supercilious attitude, and your rotten taunts, and your rotten aspirin bottle—and—and—get your hands off me——!'

The rest of her words were muffled against the hard wall of his chest as he dragged her unceremoniously away from the fragments of pottery on to the sheepskin rug. One arm clamped her waist, while his free hand exerted a firm, restricting pressure at the nape of her neck.

'Just this once I'll ignore that display of temper,' he told her coolly. 'I dare say things haven't gone too well for you today.' He gave her a narrow-eyed glance. 'You aren't accident-prone, are you? Wrecking your car is one thing, but if you're going to set about demolishing my house as well——'

'If I were,' she retorted, sniffing, 'I'd make darned sure I made a better job of it than this.'

'That figures,' he said with a grimace. 'Though with any luck you'll be about as successful as you were when you tried to sabotage the Ashford project.'

Kim scowled darkly, and shifted away from him, sliding down on to a broken piece of china. Her teeth sank into her lip, and then she was hauled on to his jean-clad thighs, her cheek brushing wetly against the bare skin of his chest.

He looked down at her, his mouth twisting. 'I guess your biorhythms are just about as screwed up as they can be. What you need is to unwind a little, learn a few relaxation techniques.' He eased his weight further on to the soft fleece of the rug, and she gave a hysterical kind of hiccup.

'How would you know what anyone needed?' she muttered. 'You don't have a sensitive bone in your body. You're nasty, devious, bad-tempered; anyone with half a——'

His fingers came to rest on her mouth, shutting off the flow of words. 'You're obviously still in shock,' he said smoothly. 'Don't say anything you might regret later.'

Her teeth snapped together in resentment. Better that his finger had been in the way, she thought sourly, but her luck was out. She pulled a face and jerked against the restraining clamp of his arm.

Drawing in a breath, she hissed, 'I know perfectly well what I'm saying. I've never met anyone so arrogant, self-opinionated—uh——'

His mouth clamped down on hers, effectively cutting off the rest of her speech, and smothering the protest that tried to surface. The hard pressure of his mouth was unexpected; her mind skittered, her senses reeled in wild disarray.

She fought him then, twisting to free herself from the hold he had on her, and he pushed her back on to the rug, trapping her beneath him with his hard, lean body. Her robe shifted with the movement, and she turned to cover herself.

His hands stopped her, warm and strong, pinioning her to the ground, and she moaned softly as his fingers brushed her tender flesh.

His head lifted, and for a moment he looked into her face. Then, drawing aside the folds of her robe, he discovered for himself the harsh, reddening line that marred her skin.

Her skin tingled where he had touched her, but it was not from pain that she whimpered. It was the dangerous beguilement of that sensuous, silken touch that made her pulses leap.

Kim felt a rush of heat and cold all at the same time as he stared down at her. She felt the glittering sweep of his blue eyes flame over the once creamy translucence of her skin in the seconds before his mouth descended to make a lingering exploration of the curve of her shoulder.

His warm breath lightly fanned her throat, and then, without warning, his tongue edged sideways to slide, feather-light, over her bruised flesh. She began to tremble uncontrollably as his lips followed a slow journey of discovery along that dark line, down towards the rounded slope of her breast. The denial that quivered on her tongue clung thickly, swallowed up in the thrum of her own pulse that sounded discordantly in her ears.

The caress was having a disturbingly hypnotic effect on her body, and she clung to the last scrap of her failing resistance. Without it, she was lost. The warmth of his body, permeating through the denim to her legs, made her all too aware of him, of his vital strength.

She gave a small sob of dismay, moving beneath him, and his blue eyes shifted to the shapely line of her bare thigh, and continued to roam idly.

Suddenly, she found the strength to push him from her, tearing herself out of his grasp. Shakily, she got to her feet, pulling the robe about her. What on earth was she thinking of? Where had she left her wits? The horror of how nearly she might have succumbed to the subtle invitation of his embrace engulfed her.

Greg stood up, looking her over, and she glared at him fiercely. He of all people was a man she should be fighting; how could she have forgotten so easily? Where was her loyalty to Steve? This man had ground him underfoot, and she had almost—— Shame swamped her, cutting off the thought.

'I'm going back to bed,' she told him. 'In the morning, as soon as the main roads have been cleared, I'm leaving.'

'I see,' he murmured. 'And how are you proposing to get through the drifts to the main road?' The enquiry was deceptively mild.

'I'll walk.'

Greg let his glance wander to her bare feet. Of course he knew that her shoes would be woefully inadequate. 'Fine,' he said, the cynicism in his voice making her edgy. 'Just as you like...' He paused. 'I wonder, though, just what it is that you're running away from?' His brow lifted. 'Me? Or could it be the fact that you can't trust yourself not to fraternise with the enemy?'

CHAPTER FIVE

KIM'S breath caught sharply at the deliberate thrust. She felt the blood drain from her face, and the world tilt and slide in a way that made her feel sick and dizzy. 'Fraternise with the enemy'. Greg's words had been cruel, designed to hurt, and he had known exactly how to turn the knife for maximum effect. But wasn't it the truth? Wasn't that exactly what she had been doing? The thought appalled her.

She made herself stare coolly into his eyes. It took a great deal of effort to put on a show of unconcern, but she could not bear to let him think he had scored a hit.

'Enemy?' she repeated, raising a delicately arched brow. 'You flatter yourself if you believe our short acquaintance merits such a depth of feeling. In fact, Mr Coulter, I have absolutely no thoughts about you one way or the other.'

Scooping up a couple of pills, she turned away from him and made her way up the stairs without once looking back. She did not want to see the mocking glint that would be in his eyes. It was enough that he plagued her to distraction, without giving him the satisfaction of thinking he had succeeded in nettling her.

In her room, she went over to the small vanity unit, and poured cold water into a glass. She swallowed the tablets and put the glass back on the shelf with a determined clink, staring at her flushed face in the oval mirror. Now that she was alone, her skin burned with the humiliation of the last few hours, and she turned on the tap and splashed her cheeks with cool liquid, savouring the relief it brought.

After only a short time in his company, she had come dangerously close to relaxing her guard, and who could tell what might have happened if she had not come to her senses? He had kissed her to keep her quiet—that had been his only motivation.

That she had so nearly responded, that her body could betray her so easily, was something she did not like to dwell on. She would have to keep well clear of him in future, for her own peace of mind. He was definitely a man to avoid.

First thing in the morning, she promised herself, she would get away from here. No matter what he said, or what difficulties that decision presented, she had to go, as soon as was humanly possible. With that thought, she climbed into the big bed and sank almost immediately into an exhausted sleep.

It was some hours later, when the weak sun slipped through the chinks in the curtains, and danced lightly over her eyelids, that Kim blinked and stirred lazily. For a few moments she gazed around the unfamiliar room before she realised where she was, and then, as the memories came flooding back, she hurriedly pushed the quilt from her and slid her legs out of bed.

She washed and dressed quickly, amazed to find that her head was reasonably clear, though tender to the touch, and apart from a stiffness about her shoulders she was more or less back to normal. Her mouth shaped a grim smile. Greg Coulter had better watch his step. If he thought she was going to be easy to manipulate, he would have a shock coming. Now that she was fully recovered, there would be no haziness around the edges of her thinking. Her defences were activated and registering red alert.

The smell of frying bacon met her as she went downstairs, but it did little to mollify her abrasive mood. The thought of having to share breakfast with Greg Coulter did not sit easily with her.

He turned from the cooker as she walked into the kitchen. He said briskly, 'See to the coffee, if you want one. This is about ready. Do you want toast?'

She eyed the food moodily. 'I'm not hungry.' Her glance went to the window, and the snow-covered ground outside.

'Suit yourself,' he said. 'You'll be the one to suffer. There's no knowing how long it will be before we get away from here.'

'The snow-ploughs will have been out,' she muttered, as she sat down and reached for the coffee-pot. 'The main roads are bound to be clear by now.'

Greg said nothing, but his lips stretched, showing his white teeth, and her grey eyes, smoky with resentment, met his. He was enjoying this, she fumed inwardly. He knew exactly how she felt. She looked away, glowering into her coffee-cup.

A plate of bacon and fritters was pushed towards her, and she sensed that he was waiting for her to refuse it. Picking up a fork, she began to jab irritably at the food.

They ate in silence. Out in the hall, the telephone began to ring, and, without haste, Greg finished the last morsel of food on his plate before getting to his feet.

How could he be so relaxed, so sure of himself? Kim frowned at his retreating back, and he turned and caught her glare. A faint smile tugged at his mouth as he lifted the receiver.

'Helen, how are you?' Through the open door, she saw that he was still smiling, and his voice reflected his amusement.

Kim bent her head and pushed the remains of her breakfast around her plate, trying not to listen to his conversation. His love-life was his own concern. It didn't interest her in the least. She didn't even like the man.

An unfamiliar tightness gripped her stomach. What did it matter to her that this woman called him at the office and knew his private number? He was welcome to her. The only reason she felt out of sorts was because she had been through a difficult weekend. It was enough to make anyone feel queasy. Hearing his affectionate tone as he spoke to the woman just added to the nausea.

Lifting her coffee-cup to her lips, she caught sight of her white knuckles gripping the rim, and forced herself to relax. It was the knowledge that she was forced to endure the company of a man who had no scruples that was making her so edgy.

What would this Helen think of his actions last night? No doubt he would keep this weekend quiet. Her eyes slitted. He wanted an easy life, with no trouble to ripple the waters.

Her glance travelled to the hall, flickering over his strong, lean frame. The sleeves of his shirt were rolled back to reveal tough, sinewy fore-arms, his wrists hard-boned, his long fingers firm on the receiver.

'The forecast isn't good,' he was saying, 'but the main roads might be clear by now. Don't worry; I'll do my best to get back.'

Finishing the call, he came back into the kitchen, and went over to a small cloakroom, where he unhooked a warm, fleece-lined jacket from a peg, and then pulled on a pair of sturdy boots.

'I'm going to clear the snow from the drive,' he said. 'That should suit your prickly hide well enough.'

He went off in search of a spade, and Kim began to stack the plates and cups in the dishwasher. She knew a perverse feeling of resentment as she watched him preparing for their journey home. Who was this woman who could get him to race back to her at a mere word? The dishes clattered into the wire racks.

Greg came back into the room just as she was slamming the door shut on the pots with undue force. 'Something wrong?' he queried, raising a black brow.

She said tautly, 'Nothing at all. Don't let me keep you from your shovelling; I'd hate us to be stranded in another blizzard.'

He looked at her thoughtfully. 'Do I take it you're claustrophobic as well as accident-prone? Is there anything else I should know about? I'd like to be prepared.'

'The only thing that you need to know is that I want to get away from here, and away from you, as fast as possible.'

'Really? Why the desperate rush to escape? Did I tread on a nerve somewhere last night? Were you afraid you might actually begin to loosen up a little and look forward to an illicit weekend? Is that why you panicked?'

He walked towards her, slowly, his eyes dark, glittering over her stiff form. 'Perhaps you've had a change of heart. Has disappointment and frustration set in overnight? What am I supposed to do—remedy the situation?'

'Stay away from me,' she hissed through her teeth. 'I don't need you and your oversized ego, and your cracks about my sex-life. I'm…already involved with someone, so you can leave me alone.'

It was a lie. The only man in her life was Richard, and her relationship with him was nothing more than a long-standing friendship. She had wanted to put Greg down quickly, but, much as it would have pleased her to do it, she wasn't strong enough to punch him on the jaw. Words were the only weapon she had.

His mouth twisted with scorn. 'You—involved? Don't make me laugh. No one could be in the middle of a relationship and still have that lacing of frost around the edges, unless the man's a total android.' He turned away from her and went out into the ice-laden air.

Recovering herself belatedly, Kim scowled at his retreating figure in cold, impotent fury.

It was some three hours later, after a journey made in almost complete silence, that he drew the car to a halt outside the unprepossessing terraced villa where she lived. Kim turned to him and said thinly, 'I won't offer you coffee. I've no doubt you have to be off somewhere?'

His glance shifted from the grey stucco of the house to rest on her cool features. 'You're quite right. I promised Helen I'd meet her as soon as we arrived back.'

Kim gave a brief nod. Helen; of course. The man had no principles whatsoever. Or did he put down last night's skirmish to one of expediency?

Gathering her belongings together, she slid out of the passenger seat, unhappily conscious of the heavy knot of tension tightening her stomach. It was her dislike for him that was causing it, she told herself. There was no valid reason for her to feel this resentment. It was her capricious mind playing devilish tricks. She was not at all disturbed by the fact that he had women friends. Just the opposite—hopefully while he was occupied with them he would not be tormenting her.

As she started up the steps which led to the main door, he said, 'Have your notes typed up and on my desk within the next two or three days. I want to make a start on this one as soon as possible.' He did not wait for an answer, and she heard him drive away, the engine of his car purring smoothly into the distance.

Her face set into mutinous lines. He wanted a miracle-worker, not an architect. Two days... to absorb all the information she had collated, and come up with some visionary ideas—that was what he meant, but it was impossible. That was why he had made the demand, of course. He did not believe she could do it. Her mouth firmed. She would show him.

She paused at the porch, searching in her bag for her key. The house was old, and had been converted into smaller apartments a couple of decades before. That the landlord had done next to nothing to improve the condition of the property since then was patently obvious from the peeling frontage. She wondered what Greg must have thought of it, then shrugged dismissively. He moved in far different circles from her own. Thank goodness.

Kim took her work home with her over the next two evenings, and worked well into the late hours. She was determined to come up with some brilliant ideas that would hit Greg Coulter for six. The plans for the Ashford development were not far off completion, for all that he had complained, and she felt fairly confident that she could set them aside for a few hours without any harm.

On Wednesday morning she switched on her coffee-percolator and blew a fuse which promptly put out all the lights in the flat. Frowning in exasperation, she made up her mind to give her landlord a ring later that day, and finished getting ready for work in semi-darkness. She was always pushed for time in the mornings, and today was no exception. Last-minute mishaps were the last thing she needed.

Making a dash for the bus, she reflected that not having the car was proving to be a real nuisance, although with a bit of luck that should be remedied soon.

She ran all the way from her stop to the impressive Coulter Construction building, and hurried into the office, arriving slightly winded, and pink-cheeked from her exertions.

The phone was ringing as she walked to her desk. Sliding into her chair, she lifted the receiver.

'Hello?' She ran a hand through her hair, and looked up to see Greg frowning at her from the doorway. She grimaced. Why did he always have to appear at inopportune moments? Turning away from his dark-eyed scrutiny, she said huskily, 'Richard, this is a surprise. Is everything OK?'

Richard's voice held a note of regret. 'I'm afraid something's come up, and I have to go to London later today. It means I'll have to call off our meal for this evening. I'm really sorry, Kim; I was looking forward to it.'

'Don't let it bother you.' She gave a rueful laugh. 'The way things are going we would have had to eat out anyway.'

'Are you still having problems with the flat?' he queried sympathetically.

'One or two,' she agreed, 'though I dare say it will be sorted out eventually.'

'You could always come and stay at my place,' Richard told her. 'There's a spare room, and you know you're more than welcome any time you want—you've only to say the word. I can let you have a key.'

She thought for a moment. 'Thanks,' she murmured hesitantly. 'I might take you up on that.'

Conscious of Greg's frigid stare, she said, 'I'll let you know what I decide to do,' and, after a moment or two, brought the conversation to an end. Putting the receiver carefully back on its rest, she swivelled around in her chair to face him.

He smiled unpleasantly, his teeth gritted. 'Oh, you've finished, have you? Perhaps now we could get some work done around here.'

She flushed at the abrasive sarcasm of his tone, but returned his hostile scrutiny without flinching. 'Did you want me for some reason?' she enquired, her mouth clamped.

'If it isn't too much trouble,' he said coldly. 'I hate to intrude on the vastly important arrangement of your personal affairs, but if you could spare a moment or two I'd like to know how far you've gone with your notes on the business park.'

'I'm working on it,' she told him, keeping a tight control on the brittle emotions that seethed just beneath the surface of her cool exterior. 'You should have the typed-up documents by, say, this evening.' Even if she had to work through her lunch-break and do overtime, she'd see to it, she thought grimly.

He frowned, his thick, dark brows coming together in a hard line. 'I doubt I shall be back by then,' he told her, his voice clipped. 'I've a lunch appointment, and I'll probably be out of the office for the whole of the afternoon.' He stood thinking for a moment, his lips drawn back against his teeth, his breath hissing slightly through them. Abruptly he said, 'Get the papers up to my office as soon as you have them ready.'

Kim resisted the temptation to give a smart salute and reply sharply, 'Yes, sir,' contenting herself instead with making a slow count to twenty under her breath as he strode briskly out of the room. The door slammed shut behind him.

Kim directed a brooding stare at the door. It felt as though an arctic wind had just blown through the room.

Coming in from the outer office, Mike Jennings enquired frowningly, 'Was that the boss? What's rattled his cage?'

'I can't imagine,' Kim muttered. 'Who can tell what makes his mind tick?'

'I dare say this Masters business could be at the back of it,' Mike murmured, deep in thought. 'So far he's managed to keep him from doing anything hasty, but, if the situation changes for the worse and Masters withdraws from the contract, it's bound to be bad for business.'

'There's not much chance of that, is there?' Kim said with an edge of bitterness. 'He already has Steve's head on the block for that mess. The fact that he's an innocent party doesn't seem to cut any ice at all.'

Mike made a wry smile. 'That may be, but Masters was touchy enough to begin with about Coulter's involvement with his wife—it was only the fact that Coulter Construction is a big name around here, and the price was highly competitive, that encouraged him to go ahead with the deal.'

Kim's head flicked upwards, her eyes wide with shock, a wave of sickness making her stomach flip over. 'His wife? But surely...'

'Didn't you know?' Mike shrugged. 'I thought it was common knowledge around here. There used to be a big thing going on between Helen Masters and Coulter at one time. In fact...' he paused, frowning '...I think they were engaged, but something went wrong and she married Alan instead.'

Kim stared blankly in front of her. Helen? Helen Masters? The woman that Greg had been in constant touch with over the last few weeks? The same woman who had called him at his weekend cottage?

'I've a feeling,' Mike went on, 'that she's his lunch appointment. She came in here first thing, and went straight up to his office. I should think he'll have to watch his step there—it would only take one spark for the whole set-up to flare up in his face.'

Kim felt the nausea grip at her midriff, and leaned forward in her chair to ease it.

'Are you all right?' Mike asked. Her forehead felt damp, tiny beads of perspiration breaking out on her smooth skin.

She nodded, and he said quietly, 'I shouldn't let his bad temper get to you. Most likely it will all blow over in a day or two.'

'You're probably right,' she muttered. Was it Greg's foul mood that bothered her? Would that account for the sudden churning sensation that had taken her by storm? Lately her emotions were in such a tangle, she didn't know what to think any more.

She pulled her folder of notes towards her, and Mike must have taken it as a sign that all was well because he gave her an encouraging smile and went back to his own desk.

Kim looked unseeingly at the papers in front of her. Could it be true that Greg was involved with a married woman? What kind of man was he? Maybe there was an innocent explanation for his meetings with Helen Masters? Perhaps she had misconstrued the situation, imagined that it was something more than it really was. She bit down on the soft inner flesh of her lip. Why did she care so much about the answer?

Mike moved over to the filing cabinet and pulled open a drawer, bringing her wandering thoughts to a jolting stop. Kim blinked. There had to be some way of getting Greg out of her head, she decided, picking up a thick black pencil and dragging a sheet of notes from the file towards her. Putting her ideas into some kind of order would be a start.

Over the last few days she had come up with several ideas for the Derbyshire enterprise, and she spent the rest of the day fining them down into a workable proposition. Lunch was a quick sandwich eaten at her desk and washed down with coffee from the machine. She was typing out a neat copy when Mike leaned over and said, 'I'm off now. Are you about through?'

Startled out of her preoccupation, Kim glanced down at her watch. She had not realised it was so late.

'Oh . . . bye, Mike. I hadn't noticed the time.' She waved a hand at the folder on her table. 'This is about finished now, so I think I may as well stay on and add the last touches to the Ashford project. With luck, Greg might be so amazed he'll be dumbstruck for the next week or two, and then we'll all get some peace.'

Mike laughed. 'Don't work too hard, will you? You don't want to take the boss's badgering too seriously, you know. You're only flesh and blood. There's a limit to what you can do.'

She smiled ruefully. 'I wonder if he knows that.' With a soft sigh, she stretched her limbs. 'Anyway, it shouldn't take too long. There are just one or two things I have to check from the files in his office, then I can close it up and forget about it.'

'That's good,' Mike said. 'I'll see you in the morning, then.'

The office was quiet when he had gone, and she spent another hour looking through the Ashford papers before she slipped them into a file and made her way up to Greg's office. The building seemed to be deserted now; there was a hollow, empty ring to the place as she went through the foyer to the lifts, though she supposed that the security man would be around somewhere.

Greg's office was familiar to her by now, and she went over to the filing cabinet that stood against one wall. Mandy usually produced any documents that were needed from the drawer at the top, and now Kim pulled it open, flicking quickly through the various dividers until she found the check-list she was searching for. Pulling it out, she skimmed through it, then copied the information she needed on to one of the papers in her folder. It was finished. A feeling of well-being swept over her, like a warm tide, as she slipped the document back into the drawer.

But the warmth did not last. It ebbed away as her glance was drawn towards a letter which had been neatly filed away in a clear plastic wallet. Slowly, the contents filtered through to her brain.

At first the figures meant nothing to her, then, as the truth dawned, she recognised what it was that she was seeing. The letter was in reply to a query from Greg about a contract that he was interested in securing. The writer listed the various prices already put in by other competitors for the job, and went on, 'We will look forward to receiving a favourable estimate from you within the next fortnight.'

Kim lifted the letter out of its wallet, and stood transfixed, staring down at the paper. Richard had been right all along. This was how Greg managed to slide contracts from under the noses of his rivals. All he had to do was put in a lower quote than those already tendered, and the work was his.

A muted drumming started up in her ears. She felt slightly dizzy. Behind her a low, muffled tread on the carpet made her turn, and she looked up into Greg's faintly narrowed eyes.

'Working late?' he queried softly.

Her throat was tight, and her voice, when it came, was roughened. 'I didn't expect you back today.'

'I can see that.' His glance flickered over the letter drooping from her hand. 'What are you looking for, in particular? Is it anything I can help you with?'

'I needed to look at the list of suppliers for the Ashford project.'

He said evenly, 'Your search must have gone astray somewhat. That doesn't look like it to me.'

'No.' Kim's mouth made a bitter line. Her grey eyes were smoky with accusation. 'But very interesting, all the same.'

Greg pushed the door shut behind him. A muscle flicked in his jaw. 'Is that so? Then it would appear that now might be as good a time as any to talk about it.'

CHAPTER SIX

'WHAT is there to discuss?' Kim looked at Greg with open hostility. 'It all seems very clear to me. In fact, I'd say the evidence was quite damning, wouldn't you agree?' She waved the letter in front of him, cutting the air with it. 'No wonder you get the lion's share of the contracts that come on the market.' A wave of bitterness swamped her. There could be no doubt of his unscrupulous determination to ride roughshod over everyone else. He had to win; that was all that mattered to him.

'The proof of the kind of man you are is written there, in black and white.' She flicked the paper with the back of her hand. 'You don't care that people are trodden underfoot, that they could go out of business, just as long as you get what you want. That's all that interests you, isn't it?'

His eyes scanned the paper briefly. He said, 'You think that being aware of the prices other firms have put in is not ethical?' He shrugged. 'That sort of thing goes on all the time. You're being naïve if you think otherwise.'

Her spine stiffened. 'You're the one who mentioned ethics. I'm surprised you've even heard the word. All you can think of is grabbing con-

110

tracts from under the noses of others. Obviously the morality of the situation doesn't come into it as far as you're concerned, just as long as you can achieve your aim. You must have the system neatly sewn up to your own advantage.'

'And if I have?' His gaze narrowed on her. 'What are you going to do about it?'

Kim's head went back at the open provocation in his tone. He believed he was safe, that there was no way she could harm him. She'd dearly love to pull the carpet from under him.

'That would depend,' she said tautly, 'on what your next move is. Let's just say that I don't intend to sit back and let a member of my family come to any harm at the hands of a ruthless human juggernaut.'

Leaning against the door, he assessed her with cool speculation, his arms folded across his chest. Silkily, he enquired, 'Have I understood your meaning? Are we talking deals here?' Kim's chin jutted belligerently. 'Let me guess...' he said '...you keep quiet, and in return I reinstate your stepfather...is that how it goes?' Her gaze remained steadfast.

'And if I choose not to?' he murmured. 'What happens then?'

Tight-lipped, she said, 'I'm sure your competitors would be curious to know what has been going on. Richard Villiers, for instance. He would only need to undercut your price by a small amount and your profit margin would start to suffer a nasty set-back.'

'Villiers...' Cold blue eyes shifted over her, his mouth hardening. 'You know him?'

She nodded. 'Richard and I go back a long way. I told you I had contacts.'

'So you did. He was the one who phoned you this morning, I suppose. How very cosy.' He was silent for a moment, frowning in concentration, then he said tersely, 'At least now things are beginning to add up. I guess you've been roped in to help out with a little obstruction here and there from the inside, haven't you? Villiers was always trying to find ways to get back at me for firing him. Was this whole thing some kind of family enterprise? First of all the stepfather, and now...the lover?'

He said this last with a faint sneer, and she sucked in her breath sharply through her teeth. 'You've no right to talk to me like that,' she gritted.

His brow quirked sardonically. 'I don't see why not. You've had more than enough to say to me when it suited you.' He stared at her, grim-faced. 'You don't like the fact that I've cottoned on to your budding conspiracy—well, that's too bad; you should have been more careful if you didn't want to get your fingers burned.'

There was the thread of cold anger in his tone, a harsh undercurrent that made her skin prickle. Kim shot him a guarded look from under her

thick gold lashes. She did not like the way his
voice had altered, and she was disturbingly conscious of the glitter that sparked fitfully in his
eyes. It spelt danger, and she was all too aware
that he had not yet moved from the door, was,
in effect, barring her exit.

Curtly he said, 'How long have you been in
league with him? Did it start even before you
came to work for me? Is that why you chose this
firm?'

She strove to shake off the feeling of apprehension that was creeping through her. He did
not like to think that anyone could oppose him,
but she would stand her ground. She would not
let him browbeat her.

'Of course,' she answered with asperity. 'That's
why I wanted to leave at the first opportunity.'

He shook his head, ignoring her sarcasm. 'I
think not. The truth is, I had found you in my
house and you thought the plot had been rumbled
and a quick get-away was in order.'

Kim glared at him. 'I told you why I was there.
You're just twisting everything around to hide
your own guilt. It wasn't enough that you jack-
booted your way over your competitors—you
wanted to make a pile of money out of the
Masters contract as well, and you weren't too
particular how you went about it. You were put
on the spot when he found out what you were
up to, weren't you? So you covered yourself by
making Steve take the rap for everything that was

wrong.' She flung the words at him, like sharp, angry darts, but immediately they were out of her mouth she regretted them. She had gone too far. She saw that, with sickening clarity. His face set into granite lines, his features darkening with grim purpose.

He started towards her, and she began to back away warily, until her hips came up against the edge of the table and there was nowhere else to go, except sideways. Her glance travelled to the door, flickering nervously as she sidled to her left.

'I wouldn't advise it,' he warned, halting her, his voice low and deadly, his hands closing on her arms. 'You and I still have some talking to do.' Her breath caught in her throat, the air in her lungs constricting.

She tried to move, but his fingers clamped the tender flesh of her arms, pulling her towards him so that his long, hard body threatened hers, making her acknowledge his lean, muscled strength. It made her dizzy, that recognition of his fierce, powerful masculinity; it brought the blood rushing to her head in a swift, violent flood.

'You should have been taken in hand a long time ago,' he muttered harshly. 'How you can have the gall to accuse me of such a catalogue of crime is beyond my comprehension. What gives you the right to sit in judgement on me?'

'I'm only stating facts,' Kim told him. 'If the truth hurts, that's your problem, not mine.'

'You're wrong. You've involved yourself in my affairs, and that gives you a lot to answer for. I wonder,' he murmured silkily, 'what it was that you expected to gain from hassling me? Was it meant to be some kind of revenge because I had the temerity to sack Villiers? Did you think, between the three of you, that you might drag my company to its knees?' His mouth twisted. 'A rather futile ambition, wouldn't you agree?'

He seemed to move even closer, and Kim did not reply, intimidated by his tough, unyielding frame and the hidden menace threading his words. She swallowed distractedly and his hand stole up to close around her throat, his thumb coming to rest in the vulnerable hollow at its base.

'You're taking a treacherous path, Kim,' he warned her softly. 'Opposing me will be a big mistake.' Silver light glimmered coldly in the depths of his blue eyes, and Kim shivered. The tip of her tongue flickered over lips that were suddenly very dry.

'Am I making you nervous?' he murmured, watching her closely. 'You know, I think I'm glad about that.' His thumb moved slowly over the softness of her skin.

She bit down on her inner lip. 'Take your hands off me,' she demanded shakily, her grey eyes wide. She struggled against him in a vain attempt at escape. His body held her prisoner. Desperation invaded her voice. 'You can't manhandle me this way.'

'That's Villiers's prerogative, is it?' Greg's stare bored into her, savage, intensely blue, and she flinched.

'Mind your own business,' she grated.

His lips moved in a cruel smile. 'That's exactly what I am doing,' he said, shaking her so that her head rocked back and forth like a rag doll, and her teeth chattered painfully.

'Let me go,' she bit out, her breath coming in short gasps.

'When I'm ready.' He scoured her features, contempt etched into the rigid line of his jaw. 'Do you think you can get away with anything you like, say what you want without any reper-cussions? Well, let me tell you, lady, there comes a point when you have to pay for your actions.'

She was conscious of the fingers that still held her, pressurising her tender skin. A pulse beat frantically in her throat, choking her with its intensity.

'You can't threaten me,' she said hoarsely. 'There's nothing you can do.'

'Don't you believe it,' he rasped, and her eyes widened at what she saw in his face.

A soft, incoherent sound quivered on her lips, and he stared down at the pink, full curve of her mouth, shadows darkening his eyes.

'Maybe the time for talking is past,' he mut-tered thickly. 'Perhaps there's only one way to get through to you.'

Too late she read his intention, and her evasive action came to nothing as his head bent, and his mouth fastened on hers. His lips took what she tried to deny, taking possession of her with forceful demand. He kissed her with a mind-shattering, bruising thoroughness that drained her of resolve, of the strength to fight. Heat rose in her in a slow, drugging spiral, as his fingers moved over her shoulders and down her back, smoothing over the silk of her blouse, making tantalising circles along the delicate bones of her spine. Her limbs were fluid, melting, a shuddery breath quivered against her rib-cage.

His seeking hands registered the tremor, and he was still for a moment before his fingers slid around to cup the soft fullness of her breast. She tried to draw back, but his thumb brushed the turgid peak, and a moan caught sharply in her throat, exquisite tension coiling in her as he made a slow, sensual exploration. She made to writhe away from him, but he moved with her, compelling her against the broad expanse of his chest, so that her senses were filled with him, with his strong, overt masculinity.

'No...' The word was muffled, swallowed up by his questing lips. He pressured her to yield to the hot demand of his mouth, his tongue flickering hungrily, searching out the secrets she tried to keep from him. A tremor of unbidden, aching desire started up in her and began to spread in ever widening circles through her body.

She was bewildered by the conflict that raged inside her. How could she want him? How could her body betray her so easily with a man she ought to despise, a man who could destroy her, a man who was already involved with someone else?

She jerked away from him, her palms flattening in rejection on the solid, muscled band of his chest. 'No...' she said again, the word a harsh, discordant sound. Her hands lifted to ward him off. 'Don't touch me.'

She stared at him, stricken, her grey eyes brilliant with the shimmer of unshed tears. 'I thought I knew what kind of man you are, but I hadn't even begun to plumb the depths. You think you can have it all your own way, but, believe me, you've reached the end of the line. You're going to come unstuck.'

He was very still, watching her, waiting. He said, 'Am I? Would you mind telling me how, and why?'

Her mouth shaped her bitterness. 'I should have thought you could work it out for yourself. You've been playing a dangerous game, but sooner or later it's going to come to an end. Haven't you considered how Alan Masters might react to your exploits? So far, your main concern has been that he would object if you reinstated my stepfather. What do you expect he will do when he discovers that you've been messing around with his wife?'

'What——?' The sound exploded from him like a bullet from a gun. He took a deep breath. 'What did you say?'

On firmer ground now, Kim viewed him with scorn. 'Did you think I didn't know? You should have covered your tracks a bit more carefully if you wanted to keep it a secret. As it is, he might well consider pulling out of the contract and looking elsewhere if he hears the rumours about your liaison.'

'What are you talking about?'

Kim shrugged. 'Word gets around. And you haven't exactly been discreet. There are the phone calls to begin with,' she informed him coolly. 'And not just to the office—she even has the number of your hideaway, for heaven's sake. Not to mention all the lunch-dates and——'

'Business meetings.' He slashed the words at her like a scythe. 'How do you know they're nothing more than that?'

Kim smiled briefly. 'On a Sunday morning?' She lifted a finely arched brow. 'Do you really expect anyone to believe that?'

'I don't give a damn what anyone believes,' he grated. 'What I do is my affair and nobody else's. And you had better understand that. I've had just about all I'm going to take from you.' He scowled darkly. 'And while we're about it, let's get a few things clear, shall we? First, if you're so intent on bringing me down, supposition and innuendo won't even reach first base. You'll have to try for something far more substantial.'

His glance flicked to the letter that had long since fallen to the carpet. 'Second, you'll need more weaponry at your disposal than that worthless piece of paper you purloined from my files. You see, my little viper, I didn't happen to tender for that particular job. It wasn't one that I was interested in to any degree. In fact I understand it went to a new company, which specialised in factory units.'

Kim stared at him in confusion, and he went on forcefully, 'The fact that your friend Villiers missed out was entirely his own fault; it had nothing whatever to do with me. Maybe when you report back to him you should tell him to get his own house in order.'

Stark tension filled the room as their gazes locked. 'One other thing you should know,' Greg said tersely. 'Your stepfather's position here will be clarified once and for all within a week or two. Tomorrow morning, I'm going away for a few days, but as soon as I return an audit will be carried out. After that has been completed, we should be able to see clearly what has been going on.'

Kim looked at him in stunned surprise. 'But you have to find the foreman who was in charge—he's the one who can tell you all you need to know.'

Greg made a dismissive movement. 'As far as that goes, enquiries are proceeding. What is important is the result of the audit, and we shall have that soon.'

'I don't understand——' Kim began.

A muscle jerked spasmodically in his jaw. 'You're not required to understand, just to do your job.' He reached across the table for his briefcase. 'Now get out of here. I have work to do.'

Kim returned to her flat with her mind dazed by Greg's brusquely delivered bombshell. An audit. What on earth did that mean? Was there something she did not know about, some other aspect of the situation that had been kept hidden? But Steve had told her... there could not be anything else; he would have said, surely? He had been tense and anxious, but he wouldn't have left anything out, would he? It was just that Greg was being heavy-handed, searching for anything that he could pin on to the older man. He resented her interference, and he was determined to press his point home.

Her thoughts shifted restively as she entered the cramped hall and picked up the scattering of letters that awaited her. He had been so angry. Had she been wrong about him—about his affair with Helen?

She rubbed at the knot of tension that burned in her brow. Nothing had been the same since she had met Greg Coulter. Her life had been turned upside-down. Her mind, her senses, were filled with him. She did not understand how he could affect her this way—why could she not shake off this hold he had over her? She needed to free herself from this tension that had her in its grip, and maybe then her life would return to normal, to the way it had been before she had even heard of him.

Absent-mindedly, she glanced through the letters, picking out the only one which looked to be anything other than a bill or a circular. A note from the landlord. At last he had arranged for repairs and renovations to be carried out. She frowned. From the looks of things, it might be best if she found somewhere else to stay while it was going on. It wasn't likely to be very comfortable around here for a couple of weeks.

She was eating breakfast in the small kitchen next morning when the ringing of the front doorbell broke into her still troubled reflections. She wasn't used to callers this early in the day— not before she set off for work. Setting down her coffee-mug, she went to answer it, her eyes widening as she saw her car, parked at the kerb outside.

The man on her doorstep handed her the keys. 'She's good as new now. You wouldn't know she'd been in a crash.'

'But I hadn't expected it to be delivered to me—I thought someone was going to ring me and

I'd have to go along and collect it . . .' She trailed off, looking at him in happy bewilderment. 'What a relief. . . and it's all been done so quickly. I didn't think it would be fixed for at least a couple of weeks.'

'Well, there you are, that's first-class service for you. We aim to please.'

He started to move away, and Kim said quickly, 'Thank you. I imagine you'll be sending the bill through the post?'

He turned back to her, frowning. 'As far as I know, that's all been seen to. I'll check for you.' He drew a small document book from his pocket, and glanced through the crumpled pages. 'Here we are. The account was sent to a Mr Coulter, Forest Rise. It's already been settled.'

'Oh, I see.' Kim's brow furrowed. 'How much was it?'

He told her, and she absorbed the information, grimacing inwardly. 'Thank you.'

Slipping the keys into her pocket, she went back into the flat, deep in thought.

There was no way she could bear to be beholden to Greg Coulter, even for a short space of time. The money had to be returned, and straight away. Her glance went to the phone on the hall table. She would tell him that she was putting a cheque in the post. Her fingers hovered over the receiver. Glancing down at the watch on her slim wrist, she hesitated. Why was there any need for delay? There was no reason why she could not call by his house on her way to work and hand over the cheque. Of course, he might already have left on his business trip, but, if that was the case, she could simply drop an envelope through his letter-box. At least the matter would be off her conscience.

The journey to his house did not take long. It was a bright, crisp morning, with the sun sparkling over the frost-covered landscape, giving everything a brilliant, crystalline appearance. She liked the feel of the Mini; it gave her a sense of well-being to have it back.

Pulling up at the side of the road, she stepped out of the car and locked it, then started to walk along the gravelled, tree-lined drive. A sporty red MG was parked in the crescent-shaped access in front of the house, and she cast a vaguely puzzled glance over it as she pressed a finger to the doorbell. Through an open window she heard the sound of voices, one deep and definitely male, the other lighter, more melodious.

The door opened and Greg stood there, his brow furrowing as he saw who it was. From the kitchen, a woman called softly, 'Greg, darling, breakfast's ready.'

Kim froze. She recognised that voice. She had only ever heard it on the other end of a telephone, but she would know it anywhere.

'Why are you here?' Greg asked. 'Shouldn't you be at work?'

'I'm on my way,' Kim said stiffly. 'I just came by to give you this.' She held out the cheque to him, willing her hand not to shake. 'You should have given the garage my address, then you wouldn't have been inconvenienced.'

He frowned. 'It wasn't necessary for you to have made a special journey.'

'It was to me.'

Behind him, Helen Masters said, 'Shall we eat in the——?' Her glance went to the open door and flickered over Kim. She ran her hands lightly over the lapels of her silk robe. 'I didn't realise we had company.'

Kim said bleakly, 'I was just leaving. Please don't let me interrupt your breakfast.'

She turned and walked blindly back along the path. She hurt as though she had been dealt a savage blow to her midriff. He *was* having an affair with Helen Masters. His anger when she had faced him with the accusation had not been born out of righteous indignation—why had that thought ever crossed her mind? No—he had been angered only by the discovery of his sordid activities. That was why he had been put out by her appearance at his house this morning.

The physical evidence of his relationship with the other woman brought a tide of nausea welling up inside her. Stifling the sob that broke on her lips, she clamped a hand to her mouth. Why did it hurt so much? What did it matter to her what he did? Stumbling, she ran the last few yards to her car.

CHAPTER SEVEN

I DON'T give a damn what anyone believes. Greg's words came back to haunt Kim as she sat in the car, staring at the windscreen, without seeing anything. She did not start the engine; there was no way she could drive—her hands were shaking too much, and she curled them around the steering-wheel to make them still. The muscles of her stomach had tightened into a rigid band.

Her thoughts were a confused jumble, twisting and turning like the pathways of a bewildering maze, and she was lost in the middle of it, her mind numbed.

Business meetings. He had implied that there was nothing between him and Helen, and like a fool she had wanted that to be the truth. What was wrong with her? Why did she have to feel so much, when his every word and action was like a knife-thrust to her?

Angrily, she blinked away the sting of tears that blurred her vision. He had kissed her, but only because it was expedient. Most of the time he did not even like her.

A bubble of sound rose on a hysterical wave in her throat and was smothered as soon as it had begun. She swallowed hard, bitterness tugging at her mouth, and bringing with it the acrid taste of disillusion.

Despite his callous indifference, he had brought to life her dormant senses—made her want him. Why had he done that, when all the time he had Helen to warm his bed? Didn't he even care for his mistress's feelings?

Sniffing unhappily, she pressed her fingertips to her damp cheeks and thrust back the clinging strands of hair that straggled over her temples. Perhaps she had been a bigger threat to him than she imagined. Could he have been afraid that she would rock the boat, and put the contract with Masters in jeopardy? That would bring bad publicity, wouldn't it, something he wanted to avoid at all costs? He had tried to throw her off the track.

Kim took a deep, shuddery breath. She felt a profound, aching sense of loss, a pain that crept around the edges of her heart and squeezed relentlessly with cold, hard fingers.

Looking around, she gazed blankly at the green wall of shrubbery and trees that screened the house from view. Gradually, she became aware of the distant hum of traffic, of people making their way to work, the beginnings of the rush-hour. How long had she been sitting here? They were having breakfast together—how long would it be before one of them came out and discovered her still sitting here? She inserted the key in the ignition and switched on, feeling the throb of the engine as the car came to life.

She was not conscious of the route she took, and it was with a kind of shock that she found herself in the car park of Coulter Construction. The thought of being anywhere near Greg, or anything connected with him, filled her with prickling unease.

Momentarily, she hesitated, undecided whether to turn around and head for home, but then she remembered that he was going away, there was no likelihood of him coming into work that morning. Besides, she reflected sourly, he had other, more interesting things to keep him occupied.

Going into the office, she cast a dull glance over the paperwork on her desk. There was a letter from a site agent which needed her attention, some details concerning electrical work which had to be checked against the relevant sheet. She pulled the typewritten document from her drawer and looked at it without registering any of the content. The black print danced on the page before her.

The office door came open with a bang, and she jumped, sucking in her breath as Greg walked into the room, his face tightly drawn, his jaw rigid.

'You—you said you were going away,' she muttered, her tone threaded with faint accusation.

'I forgot something,' he said, eyeing her grimly.
'Any objection?'

She swallowed against the lump in her throat,
but said nothing.

He gave her a thin smile. 'What's the matter
with you?' he demanded. 'You're very pale. Is
Villiers keeping you awake too long? You'd better
tell him I'm the one who's paying you—I want
you here in the office, ready to work.
Understood?'

'Don't shout at me,' she said through her teeth.
'I've got a headache—I don't need your bad
temper.'

His brow lifted. 'Been crawling around under
his tables too, have you?'

Her fingers clenched on the paper she was
holding, and he laughed, a short, harsh sound as
he strode through to the outer room.

Tension sparked inside her, fizzing in her head
until she thought she might explode from it. Why
did she react this way? Why did she let him do
this to her?

She pressed her knuckles into the soft flesh of
her mouth. Instinct should have warned her that
any involvement with Greg would spell disaster,
yet still, insidiously, it seemed that she had been
caught up in the spell that he had woven around
her. Without her realising it, she had been drawn
ever closer to the flame, until now she was forced
to endure the scorching consequences.

It was impossible to go on working here much longer. It had been difficult before, but now she felt as though she was being torn in two. She could not bear the thought of staying here, seeing him, day after day. There were countless reasons why she should not have let her emotions get tangled up with him. Why had her heart not listened?

Her thoughts turned to Richard, and she found herself reaching for the telephone, dialling his number automatically. He had said he would help her any time, and she could do with his support right now.

He answered her call almost immediately, and she was grateful that he listened without interruption as she haltingly outlined her proposition.

'You said there might be a job for me,' she said, her fingers gripping the phone tightly. 'Does that still hold true?'

'Of course, Kim. You know I've wanted you to work with me for a long time. Don't worry about a thing. If you're not happy at Coulter's, there's always a place for you here.' His voice was deep and reassuring, and she held on to the comfort he offered as if it were a life-support.

'Thanks,' she breathed.

He said quietly, 'You don't have to thank me. You're good at your job; that's why I've been asking you to consider it all this while.'

'How are things?' Kim asked. 'Is business picking up? I don't want you to feel obliged to help me out.'

'I'm doing fine. In fact, I shall have to go abroad to look over a new enterprise after Christmas, which means the apartment will be empty. I don't suppose you'd consider my other suggestion, would you—caretaking the flat while I'm away? I'm not keen on leaving the premises unsupervised for any length of time.'

Kim thought about the letter from her landlord, and all the upheaval that there would be while the renovations were carried out.

'All right,' she agreed. 'You're on. I'm going to be in a mess in my own place when the workmen move in.' She hesitated. 'There was something else I wanted to ask . . .'

Her fingers toyed with the telephone cable as she spoke. Steve's situation worried her, and so far she had been able to do absolutely nothing for him. There might be a remote chance, though, that Richard could find Steve something if the worst came to the worst. She put it to him.

'I'm not sure, Kim,' he said at last. 'I don't have a particular slot for him at the moment, but I'll certainly see what I can do.'

She had to be satisfied with that. They settled the date for her move—a couple of days after Christmas, and Kim put the receiver down, staring bleakly at it for a moment while her nerves steadied.

She hoped he could find him a place. All her pleas to Greg had fallen on deaf ears. He had no intention of letting Steve off the hook. She made a grimace. He would hound her stepfather like an animal stalking its prey until his teeth closed on him. That was what the forthcoming audit was all about. She had to do what she could to help Steve. If Greg's plan came to fruition, she dared not think what the shock of unemployment would do to her mother. It was so unfair. Steve couldn't have done anything wrong.

She went over to the typewriter and removed its cover. Her letter of resignation would not take long to compose.

As Greg came back into the office, she looked up, her fingers resting lightly on the keyboard.

'I'm on my way now,' he informed her. 'Try not to wreak too much havoc while I'm gone. I'd like an office to come back to.'

'I'll do my best,' she muttered, getting to her feet. 'Besides, I doubt I'll be here that much longer. There are only one or two loose ends I have to clear up.'

He regarded her quizzically, and she said, 'You ought to see this before you go. That way, you can't say I haven't given you fair warning.'

She handed him the letter, and he scanned it quickly, his mouth tightening as he read the contents.

'You can't leave,' he told her curtly. 'We've been through that before. You still have to fulfil the terms of your contract.'

She gave a faint shrug. 'It makes no difference. I've decided to go, and you really have no choice but to accept it.'

'Not true, I'm afraid. I could sue, and that means you'll be out of pocket by a large amount.' His lips moved in a perfunctory smile. 'I'm sure it needn't come to that, though. We'll talk it over when I return.' He glanced down at his watch. 'I don't have time right now; I have a plane to catch.' He tore her letter in two and handed her the pieces before he left the room.

Kim stood quietly for a few minutes, watching the door that he had slammed shut behind him. Would he really go ahead with any action against her? It was a risk she had to take. She could not work with him as before; the strain would be too much and there was bound to be a breaking-point sooner or later.

Slowly, she turned, then walked back to the desk and carefully began to retype her resignation.

Four days later, Kim had just about finished wading through the hundred and one details that needed to be tied up to her satisfaction, when Mike came into the office and leaned on her table. She moved her papers to one side and sat back in her chair.

'All hell's let loose,' he said, tugging at his collar as if it was too tight. 'Lord knows what Coulter will say when he finds out.'

Kim's grey eyes lifted enquiringly. His cheeks were flushed a dull red colour, not his usual calm exterior at all.

'Masters has pulled out,' he explained quickly. 'We've lost the contract.'

Kim stiffened. 'We can't have——' She broke off, looking at him in bewilderment. 'How—why?'

Mike succeeded in wrenching his button loose. 'Officially, he says he's not happy about the way things have been carried out, but the grapevine has it that he found out about his wife and Coulter, and saw red. That was it—no more contracts with our firm, and a whole lot of murmurings among those of his cronies who have any dealings with us.'

Kim said unevenly, 'How did he know that they were . . . involved with each other?'

Mike shrugged. 'Who knows? Except I've heard that she didn't go home one night—maybe he tracked her down.'

The sick feeling came back in full force as she thought about them together. Mike's voice reached her from a distance as she struggled against the churning tide that rocked her stomach.

'The marriage has been shaky for some time—that's common knowledge. Probably, she never got over Coulter, and now she's decided that she wants him back.'

Kim cleared her things from the office that afternoon. She had done all she could to tidy up the loose ends, and she did not want to stay around any longer, in case Greg caught the next flight home.

As she was about to leave, Mike said, 'I'm giving a party for New Year's Eve. You will come, won't you? Everyone else from the office is coming. We don't want to lose touch just because you're quitting the firm.'

Kim appreciated the fact that they wanted to keep in contact, though she didn't feel much like celebrating New Year. These days she felt close to tears all the while, yet she did not know what was wrong with her. It was not as though Greg had meant anything to her, was it? She hadn't loved him. Had she?

Mike was waiting for her answer. She asked quietly, 'Will Greg be there?'

He gave a rueful smile. 'I mentioned it to him before he left, but I don't think there's much chance of him turning up—he said he might be away over the holiday period.'

That was a relief, at least. Kim said, 'I'll try to get there. Thanks, Mike.'

She would make an effort to put in an appearance at the party, if only for a short while—start the year off among friends. The old year had not been such a great success; perhaps she would have better luck with the new one.

Kim let her grey gaze roam the darkened room, shifting over the couples who were dancing in the shadows to the heavy beat of the music. Here and there, wall-lamps sent out pale golden pools of light to bathe the people who chatted idly in small, relaxed groups. The air was warm, redolent with mulled wine and spiced chicken from the buffet.

She had arrived late, after visiting her family and joining their own party for a while, but now, just before twelve, she sipped slowly at her drink, and smiled as Mike came towards her.

'Phew!' he gasped, flicking back an unruly lock of hair from his face. 'I've been waylaid at the bar for about an hour, would you believe?'

'Sounds like a tall story to me,' Kim laughed.

'It's true, I tell you. This is the first chance I've had to grab a bite to eat.' He helped himself to a sandwich from a huge platter. 'I'm glad you decided to come,' he said. 'I wondered if the thought of Greg might have put you off.' He helped himself to a sandwich from a huge platter.

'Were there any repercussions about my leaving the firm?' Kim asked.

'To say that he wasn't too pleased is putting it mildly,' Mike grinned. 'Sparks flew. Still, I expect he'll get over it soon enough. He's had time to think about it and get used to the idea. Besides, he's hardly likely to vent his anger in front of a crowd like this. I'm sure you'll be quite safe.'

'Safe?' Kim's brows met in a frown. 'Are you saying—do you mean that he's coming here, after all?'

Mike shot her a swift, worried glance. 'Didn't you know? I left a message for you——' He broke off, his eyes searching her pale face. 'Obviously it wasn't passed on; I'm sorry.'

The music stopped, and someone had switched on the radio so that the booming chimes of Big Ben sounded into the stilled, waiting atmosphere. Midnight—the old year fading and the new one just beginning. Cheering broke out, and Kim found herself caught up in the familiar round of 'Auld Lang Syne', the hugs and kisses of friends.

Breathlessly she turned, and it was then that she saw him, across the room, his broad, muscular figure unmistakable in the darkness. Kim's lungs constricted painfully.

He stood apart from the general mêlée, his searching gaze sweeping the heads of the assembled revellers until he found her. His eyes locked with hers, and narrowed, dark as obsidian. The line of his mouth was firm and unyielding, the angle of his jaw taut. He began to move, and panic filled her, leaping wildly in her chest as he came towards her, his wide shoulders forcing an easy path through the chattering groups of guests.

She did not wait to argue with the grim purpose she read in his rigid features. She swung round and began to push her way through the thronging, laughing mass of people, the one thought uppermost in her mind, escape. She headed through the arched opening which led from the lounge and out into the dining-room, where only a few people were gathered, mostly around the buffet, picking at the remains of the food.

Greg's voice stopped her, low and gritty, a determined edge to it. 'I want to talk to you.'

She threw him a quick, dismissive stare. 'That's a pity, because I don't have anything to say to you. My letter said it all.'

Without a backward glance, she turned and went towards an open doorway. At the back of her mind, she carried the thought that the taxi she had ordered might, by some scarcely conceivable stroke of fortune, arrive early, and she could get away from him.

She made it as far as the hall before she felt the clamp of his strong fingers on her arm. 'This has nothing to do with your letter,' he told her tersely.

The door to the study was open, and he pushed her into the empty room, kicking the door shut behind him. He did not let her go.

Striving for a calmness she did not feel, she said, 'I don't know what you expect to achieve by these heavy-handed tactics—but I can tell you

you're wasting your time. Why don't you go and annoy someone else?'

He studied her, his eyes narrowed, glittering. 'You set me up,' he said through his teeth, 'and I want to know why. Was it something you hatched up with Villiers—or was it purely personal?'

She stared at him. 'I don't know what you're talking about,' she muttered.

'Don't give me that.' His mouth made a thin, hard line. 'When you left, you did your best to throw one last spanner in the works, didn't you? Why? I can see Villiers's motives well enough. He stood against me from the day I sacked him, and he would be only too happy to see me on a losing streak. But you, Kim—what was going on in your cold little mind? Were you scheming the whole time?'

'About what?' she asked, carefully ignoring his dark scowl.

'While you worked for me,' he told her, his voice clipped, 'you found out all you could about the contracts we were engaged on. You wanted some leverage—anything would do; it didn't matter much what it was. And you found it, didn't you? You played me along until the time was right, and then you told Alan Masters I was having an affair with his wife. You must have known that would be the last straw as far as he was concerned, that he would pull out of the contract. What was it, a fit of pique, or did the three of you get your heads together and come up with that firecracker?'

'You're crazy,' she asserted, biting her lip. 'I knew all along that you must be.'

He shook his head. 'You're the one who has the problem,' he said. 'You're suffering delusions if you imagine that losing a few contracts could break me. You have a lot to learn, Kim.'

'I haven't told Masters anything,' she said bluntly. 'If your actions have blown up in your face, you've only yourself to blame. Don't try to drag me into it.'

Greg's mouth made a cynical line. 'What gave Masters the idea that Helen had been with me? How did he find out?'

Kim lifted her shoulders carelessly. 'How should I know? Rumours have been running wild. If you want to play fast and loose, you should take more care about whose territory you stamp on.'

He watched her with brooding intensity, his eyes fixed on the rising flush that crept along her cheekbones. 'I don't believe you had nothing to do with it. You're lying. Why else would you leave? You knew that the whole thing was going to blow up; that's why you got out quickly.'

The memory of that fateful morning sent a painful jolt through Kim's chest. Her lips parted, but no sound came from them. How could she tell him that she had been blindingly jealous, that she could not trust herself not to break down and make a complete and utter fool of herself? He must never know how she felt about him. Her own wayward emotions would be a weapon for him to turn against her whenever the mood suited him.

'The work didn't suit me. I had a better offer. Now, if you'll excuse me, I want to leave.'

'Running away, Kim?' His steel-blue gaze cut into her as she struggled in vain to free herself from the heavy pressure of his hand. 'That seems to be turning into a habit with you, doesn't it?'

Kim's head lifted sharply, the silky fall of her hair rippling with the movement. She glared at him.

'It looks as though you have a few problems of your own,' she said with scathing heat, directing a scornful glance at his imprisoning fingers. 'You seem to make a habit out of man-handling me.'

His teeth bared in a feral smile, and she knew a sudden lurch of apprehension as his gaze flickered over her, becoming brilliant, burning on her skin.

He said, 'Maybe you drive me to it. You invite trouble like a cat who shows her claws and then howls when she gets them clipped.'

Flattening his palm against the small of her back, he pulled her towards him, startling the breath from her lungs. His head lowered, and he kissed her, a fierce, punishing kiss. A choked cry of denial surfaced on her lips, but he smothered

it, the fingers of his other hand tangling in the
hair at her nape, grasping her head so that she
was forced to accept his violation of her mouth.

He wanted total submission from her, she
realised, and she resisted desperately, struggling
against the treacherous weakness that invaded her
body. The marauding flick of his tongue ex-
plored the inner recesses of her mouth, and it
was all she could do to keep her lips from
yielding, to halt the betraying acquiescence of her
limbs.

Abruptly he let her go, and she swayed a little,
her equilibrium shattered by the sensual assault.
He watched her, his blue eyes glittering, and she
knew a sudden upsurge of bitterness. He wanted
only to dominate, to win. He could not bear to
be crossed in any way.

Deliberately, she wiped her mouth with the
back of her hand. 'I might have expected that
from you,' she said, forcing the words out
through her teeth. 'That's all you understand,
isn't it? You think you can take what you want,
when you want, without question.' She stared up
at him, anger tightening her features. 'I despise
you,' she breathed, 'and all that you stand for.'

His mouth twisted. 'Do you think I don't know
that? You've played it cool all along, haven't
you? I thought it was because you were an
innocent, but it wasn't that at all, was it?'

His eyes raked her, searing over her slen-
derness, the creamy shoulders left bare by the

strapless blue dress she wore, then moved down. The garment faithfully draped the curves of her body in soft, shimmering drifts of material, and his heated gaze followed every line.

Kim tugged her arm free of him, disturbed by that glinting appraisal. 'The plain truth is,' she said, her voice sharp with angry resentment, 'I don't like you, and I don't like your hands on me. I thought I had made that more than clear.'

Outside in the hall there was the sound of footsteps, and she heard Mike calling her name.

'Kim...Kim, where are you? Your taxi's here.'

She went to the door, half afraid that Greg would try to stop her, but he let her go, making no move to halt her progress out of the room.

Hurriedly, she found Mike, and said her goodbyes to her friends, heading all the time towards the door at the front of the house. A few minutes later she emerged on to the pavement.

The cold night air hit her. So, too, did the fact that Greg was out there already, talking to the taxi driver. She compressed her lips.

'If you don't mind,' she said, her tone succinct, as she went over to the car where he leaned casually, 'I have to go home.'

'Ease up, darling,' Greg murmured, his voice husky, intimate, and she realised he was acting for the driver's benefit. 'We'll go together. We can't leave things the way they are.'

She gave him a frost-laden glance. *'Darling,'* she spat through her barely parted lips, 'we can, and we will.'

Greg's mouth curved. 'You'll think differently in the morning, after we've talked. I guarantee it.'

He did not appear to have moved, yet she was suddenly aware of how close he was to her, how threatened she was by his long, powerful body. His arms closed around her, and in the next moment she protested vehemently as she found herself being lifted and bundled without ceremony into the passenger seat of the taxi. Greg's hands held her firmly, indifferent to her struggles. He gave his address to the driver.

'Don't you dare take me to his place,' she hissed at the man as he turned the key in the ignition. 'You can't let him get away with this. How do you know he's not a stranger on the make? As far as you're concerned I might not know him from Adam.'

The driver shrugged cheerfully. 'Mr Jennings said he thought you were together when he went to find you.' The car's engine fired noisily. 'I wouldn't dream of interfering,' he chuckled.

'He's paying you to do this, isn't he?' Kim seethed. 'How much is he paying you?'

Both men laughed, and Kim vented her fury in a vicious stab at her captor's ribs with the sharp end of her elbow. It made no difference to his

grip on her, and she ground her teeth in mute
rage until they arrived at his house.

Once there, when the driver was no longer
around, he dropped the act, pressuring her into
the lounge and thrusting her down on to the
couch. She sprang to her feet immediately.

'I'm going home,' she snapped. 'You can't
keep me here.'

His hands impelled her backwards on to the
velvety cushions.

'Home?' he queried, grim-faced. 'Where
would that be? Not your flat, that's for sure. You
don't live there any more, do you, Kim?'

He leaned over her, his mouth hard, a savage
anger tightening his jaw. She saw the muscle
flicking there, watched it, and realised, for the
first time, just how dangerous an opponent she
had taken on.

He said harshly, 'You didn't waste any time
before you moved in with Villiers, did you? What
did he promise you? It wasn't just a job you
traded; it had to be a whole lot more than that.'

The brooding menace of his stare filled her
with alarm, her throat closing in raw fear as he
came down beside her on the couch. His strong
limbs brushed her thigh and the satiny skin of
her bare arms. She gave an involuntary shiver.

'You found out where I went,' she stated
huskily, her throat very dry. She hadn't expected
him to do that. Not so soon.

'Of course I did,' he rasped. 'Did you think you could just disappear like that, into thin air, that I wouldn't come after you?' His mouth twisted in contempt. 'I might have guessed that Villiers was behind all this. He's been there from the beginning, hasn't he?'

'I won't be cross-examined,' she retorted, a coldness creeping through her limbs. She moved uneasily on the cushions. 'It's none of your business. I don't have to explain myself to you.'

'Ah, but that's where you're wrong, Kim,' he growled. 'You're going to tell me everything that's been going on, even if I have to wring the truth out of you.'

'You *are* crazy,' she said, looking at him in dismay. 'What am I doing here? I'm locked up with a madman.'

She tried to get up from the sofa, but he pushed her back down, keeping her there with the lean threat of his hard body. 'You're staying,' he told her with icy directness. 'Forget any idea about getting away.'

'Why?' she demanded. 'Why am I here? I've told you I had nothing to do with the Masters business.'

He said roughly, 'You were lying. There was a chance I might have been able to forgive what you did; I could perhaps have understood some of your actions. You were doing it all out of love for your family; you wanted to protect Steve, and you believed I had treated him badly.'

His eyes darkened, his voice took on a harsh, bitter edge. 'But you went to Villiers, you moved in with him, which just goes to prove that the innocent act was a sham, all of it, right from the beginning. You knew exactly what you were doing. That's what I can't stomach.'

'No.' Kim couldn't believe the way he was twisting everything. 'It wasn't like that——'

'Where is Villiers tonight?' he persisted, ignoring her protest. 'Why isn't he with you? Doesn't he know what a risk he's taking, leaving you alone?'

'Risk?' she said uneasily. 'What risk? I don't know what you mean.'

'Don't you? Are you sure? Did you think I'd just shrug and let you go after all that you've done? I warned you once before that you were making a big mistake in opposing me—you should have listened.'

He reached for her, and she struggled frantically to push his hands away, alarmed by the controlled strength she felt in his grip.

'Why are you fighting me?' he muttered. 'Don't you know it's a waste of energy?' His lips grazed her cheek, and moved down, so that she felt his breath warm on her throat.

'Don't.' It was a desperate cry, torn from her. She was afraid; she didn't recognise him in this mood. All he wanted was to conquer her spirit, to etch his domination on her soul.

'I hate you—let me go.' She twisted away from him, but he pulled her back, tethering her wrists when she would have dragged her nails down his cheeks.

'I don't believe it's hate you feel—you haven't sorted your own emotions out yet. You're too influenced by Bennett's situation to be able to see clearly. It's time the fog was cleared from your brain.'

Kim twisted her head in angry denial, and Greg's mouth claimed hers swiftly, cutting off the protest that sprang to her lips. It was a fierce, stormy possession; it made her dizzy, it made her head swim as though all her blood had rushed there at once.

He moved in closer, arching his body over hers, pinioning her beneath him with the weight of his thighs so that her soft, feminine curves were crushed against his hard, muscled length.

'I want you,' he said roughly. 'You're like a poison in my system, destroying me slowly, but I still want you, the way an addict needs a fix.'

A sob caught in Kim's throat; she was helpless in the face of the strength and determination that drove him to work out his angry frustration on her. His lips made a scorching detour along the slender column of her throat, and shifted to sear the smooth, silken nakedness of her shoulders. A low moan escaped her, warmth spreading through her limbs as his lips followed their seeking path and found the line of her bodice, where the rounded swell of her breasts burgeoned against the filmy material. Shockingly, she felt the slow glide of his tongue as he discovered the satiny texture of her skin, and a ripple of unbidden pleasure swept through her body.

'You said I was crazy,' he said, his breathing laboured as though he had run a long way, 'and it's true. You're driving me out of my head.' His heated gaze ran over the tumbled disarray of her hair, the curls spilling like spun gold over the cushions. Desire burned like living flame in his eyes as he looked down at her, and she lowered her lashes, as though that would shut out the evidence of his hunger.

His fingers went to the zipper of her dress, and he tugged at the fabric, sweeping the garment from her. She resisted, twisting beneath him, and he kissed her hard, forcing apart the soft fullness of her lips with his own.

She opened her eyes, a flush of pink riding her cheekbones as he eased back and let his smouldering blue glance move over her, touching the creamy, rose-tipped breasts with fire, sliding down to warm the smooth curve from hip to thigh.

'Don't,' she whispered, trying to cover herself. 'Please don't——'

'You take my breath away,' he muttered. 'You're so beautiful.'

Her hand brushed the hard wall of his chest, and she felt the thudding of his heart, hammering against his rib-cage.

His fingers moved to shape her breasts, his thumbs brushing like warm silk over the hardening crescents. Her flesh ached, swollen with heated arousal, and when his mouth came down to nip the turgid nipples it was almost too much to bear. She cried out, the sound wrenched from her, a soft, incoherent yearning that had to be assuaged. She ran her hands over his shoulders, feeling the hard muscles beneath her fingertips.

Greg's head lifted, and he looked at her, absorbing her restless movements, the hectic glitter of her grey eyes. His fingers slid in a tantalising arc over the sensitised nubs of her breasts and caressed each soft mound. She clung to him, shivering, excitement making her tremble, and he said hoarsely, 'I knew I could reach you. You're not so cool after all, are you?'

His hands travelled over her, enticing, seductive, each exquisite glide making her body arch with tension. 'Do you want me, Kim? Say it; tell me how much you want me.'

Her skin tingled as his fingers made faint circles over the curve of her hip and thigh. To her shame, she heard herself answer him.

'Yes—yes, I want you . . .' The words were a sob, quivering on her lips, her body poised, aching. Even knowing what he was did not alter the way she felt. She looked up at him and caught the sensual satisfaction that glimmered in his eyes. There was triumph and possession written there, and it was like a dash of ice-cold water to her senses.

This was what he had wanted all along, wasn't it—her submission, the acknowledgement of his power over her? That was all that mattered to him—power and domination.

It was not enough that he had sacked Richard, and suspended Steve; he had to win at everything. He had not liked being thwarted; when she had left that must have hurt his male pride.

She shifted, trying to avoid his stroking hand. She needed time to think, to sort out the tangle of her mind.

Greg stared at her, his eyes narrowing, a glint of silver in their depths. 'What's bothering you, Kim?'

She did not answer, and he drew her towards him, his fingers cutting into her shoulders. 'Villiers?' His jaw tightened, cynicism hardening his mouth. 'It's a little late to start thinking about him, isn't it?'

She said slowly, 'You've won—you made me admit that I wanted you; let's leave it at that—that's as far as it goes.'

'I think not.'

He was bitterly angry. Kim knew that. He blamed her for breaking up his relationship with Helen, for all the trouble over the contract—perhaps in some twisted way he wanted to vent his frustration on her. She would never be anything to him.

'You wouldn't listen to me,' she said bleakly. 'I—I tried to stop you, but you wouldn't listen.'

'You don't want Villiers,' he told her harshly. 'Why are you with him? For his money? It can't be anything else. He's not the man for you. He's too weak; he doesn't have the temperament to deal with a she-cat—he wouldn't know how to begin.'

'And you do?' she hit back, choking down a sob of frustration. 'Don't kid yourself.'

He curved his hand around her throat, and she flinched. 'I want to leave here,' she said. 'Now. I want to go home. What happened between us was just...one of those things, a—an aberration—something I want to forget.'

'You're going to find that hard to do.' He got to his feet in an abrupt movement, towering over her, his cold blue gaze raking her nakedness. Kim shivered, sick at heart, fear and despair mingled in the smoke-grey of her eyes. She reached for her dress and pulled it on with fingers that shook, aware that he watched her the whole time.

At last she stood up, facing him, her composure cracked wide open.

'What did he offer you, Kim?' Greg demanded, his voice harsh. 'How many pieces of gold did it take?'

She stared at him, pain etched into her features, and he said roughly, 'Go back to Villiers and tell him you've been naked in the arms of another man. See if he still wants you.'

She left the house, the undisguised contempt of his tone still ringing in her ears.

CHAPTER EIGHT

STEVE was pacing the floor, his movements restless and disjointed. 'I don't know how to tell you this,' he said, throwing Kim a distracted look, 'but I suppose you'll have to know some time.'

She studied him anxiously, alarmed by his haggard appearance. Normally, he was a handsome man, but now he looked ill, the skin stretched tightly over his cheekbones, dark shadows forming beneath his eyes.

'It isn't mother, is it?' she said, her voice strained. 'She hasn't had a relapse, has she?'

'No...no, it isn't that. She's just gone to the hospital on a routine visit, but I wanted to see you while she was out. I daren't let her know what's happened.'

He picked up an ornament from the shelf of the Welsh dresser, running his fingers abstractedly over its smooth surface. His hand was shaking, Kim noticed, and she worried at her lip, a desperate unease tearing at her.

He put the ornament down. 'I daren't think what it would do to her—but I just don't know which way to turn.'

Kim felt her insides knotting. 'Tell me,' she urged him. 'What's wrong, what's happened?'

She steeled herself, half guessing at what was to come, hoping that she was wrong, but knowing with a sick inner certainty that it had to do with Greg. She had spent countless sleepless nights already over him; would it never end? Did the hurt never stop?

Steve said, 'I made a mistake, Kim—a big mistake. The last few years—things have been hard. I thought I was doing the right thing, trying to get the best that I could for Maureen, things to make life easier for her, so that she didn't have to struggle. I took out a loan...' he sucked in a sharp breath, and Kim waited, watching him with apprehension clutching at her nerve-ends '...and then I couldn't keep up with the payments,' he went on. 'The mortgage on this place got out of hand, and I didn't know which way to turn. I got myself into a mess, I could feel myself going under. If Maureen found out about the debts, it would make her ill, really ill, and I couldn't risk that. In the end, the answer seemed to be staring me in the face. There was always money coming in and out of the office—payments for this and that; it wasn't always cheques—sometimes it was cash.' He paused, and Kim stared at him, her limbs beginning to feel terribly weak.

'Money?' she repeated faintly. 'Are you saying that you—stole money?'

His mouth worked convulsively. 'That's a harsh word—I...borrowed it. Just small amounts to begin with—Coulter was away so often, and he left me in charge, I had the key to the safe, I didn't think it would be noticed. I could fix the documentation without too much trouble. I was desperate that Maureen shouldn't know what was happening. I would have found a way to pay it back—I meant to do that.'

Kim felt for a chair and sat down. Her voice came out as a hoarse whisper. 'Greg didn't say anything about money being taken; he mentioned deals, things to do with the contract—there was never anything else. But that's why he brought the auditors in, isn't it?' Her eyes were wide, beseeching, wanting Steve to deny the nightmare, but he did not.

'He must have suspected all along,' Steve muttered. 'I realise that now. It was obvious that he knew fairly early on about the arrangements with the wholesalers, but I thought he might ignore that. There are nearly always backhanders to be had for using a particular product. I thought he might turn a blind eye to it, but he didn't. He didn't ignore any of it. He sacked me, yesterday. He called me into his office and told me. I'm finished, Kim; I've lost everything.'

'Is he going to prosecute?' Her fingers gripped the arms of the chair, her knuckles whitening.

'I don't know. If he does, there's no way I can keep it from Maureen.' His tone was flat, filled with defeat, and Kim was overwhelmed with a sudden flood of bitter anger.

'Surely you must have realised it would come to this? The whole idea was reckless from start to finish.'

He grimaced. 'At the time, it looked like the only option open to me. I had to do something. I didn't want Maureen to suffer.'

'No one does,' Kim muttered, 'but there are other ways of raising cash. If you'd only told me, we might have thought of a way out.'

'She'll need you,' he said wearily. 'If the worst happens, and I ... I'm sorry, Kim.'

Why had he been such a fool? Kim drove slowly back to Richard's apartment, the whole unhappy business gnawing at her mind throughout the journey. He had never done anything dishonest in his life, yet he had thrown away his reputation, his career, everything.

A weary despair weighed her down. She despised what he had done, but she understood how he had come to entangle himself in the quagmire.

There was no way out of the situation, that she could see. What he had done was wrong, and Greg had found him out. He couldn't avoid paying the price for his folly, and Maureen would pay it, too, unless Greg had a change of heart.

He wouldn't, though, would he? He had not been swayed before; he had been ruthlessly determined to do what he felt to be right, and, now that the truth was out, why should he even consider giving Steve a chance?

Her teeth snagged her lower lip. Steve's future and her mother's well-being were in Greg's hands, but how could she approach him, plead Steve's case? She had bearded the lion in his den once before, when at least she thought she had right on her side, but how could she face him now, when so much had happened between them, when she had no conviction to back her argument?

But how could she live with herself if she didn't try?

It was a minute or two after she had rung the doorbell before she heard movement coming from inside the house. Her nerve almost went— there were a few shaky seconds when she almost turned and ran, but somehow she managed to remain standing there until Greg opened the door. She had been steeling herself for this moment for the last twenty-four hours, her anxiety growing all the time.

He surveyed her in silence, his eyes watchful, narrowing on her pale features.

She swallowed hard. 'May I talk to you?' she asked, uncertainty threading her voice.

Laconically, he said, 'That depends. Is this a social visit, or have you dug up another crime that you want to pin on me?'

She moistened her dry lips. 'I came to apologise,' she said huskily.

His brows lifted at that, but to her relief he swung the door inward to allow her through.

'You had better tell me more,' he said, when they had gone through to the lounge. 'I'm not sure that I heard you correctly. Did you say apologise?'

'I heard about Steve,' she revealed quietly. 'He told me the truth about what happened.'

'Really?' He was cynical. 'What is this? Another ploy? Why pretend that you weren't in on it all along? Didn't you benefit from his thieving?'

Kim felt the blood drain from her face. 'I didn't know anything about it,' she insisted. 'He's never done anything like this before—it's totally out of character.'

Greg gave a scornful laugh, and she hurried on. 'It's true. I wanted to say that I'm sorry, I misjudged you all along—I just couldn't believe that there was any foundation to your accusations.'

He shrugged indifferently. 'So you've apologised. Whatever you say really makes no difference to the way things are.'

He went over to a cabinet and poured himself a large Scotch. Almost as an afterthought, he raised the bottle towards her, his glance questioning, and she shook her head.

'What did you expect me to do,' he said with a bite, 'say forget it, pretend it never happened?' He tilted his head back and took the whisky in one swallow, then put the glass down. 'You knew that wasn't on the cards. So what was it that you really came here for? You weren't still hoping that I would give him his job back, were you?'

'I—er——' Kim cleared her throat '—I know that what he did was——'

'Criminal...illegal...fraudulent... Why pussy-foot around?' Greg interposed harshly.

Kim took a deep breath. 'What he did was wrong, unforgivable...but there were reasons why he acted as he did——'

'Of course there were—he was greedy and he thought he'd get away with it.'

'No—he didn't want to do it, you have to understand that; there are extenuating circumstances——'

'I don't believe in extenuating circumstances. Whatever excuses he made to himself, he acted in a way which runs counter to the law—a law made to protect innocent people.'

Kim watched as he poured himself another drink. 'If you would only let me tell you why he did it, I'm sure you wouldn't feel so harshly towards him. It was because——'

'You're wasting your breath,' he interrupted coldly. 'If Bennett wants a hearing, he can crawl out from under his stone and plead his own case. He needn't bother sending a girl to do it for him.'

'It wasn't like that,' Kim denied quickly.

'Wasn't it?' Greg's angry blue gaze flicked over her. 'I can almost hear the scenario. Steve saying, "You can do it, Kim. You're an attractive woman. Play him along; he'll do anything you ask if you give him the sob treatment.'' Well, think again, lady. It won't work.'

Contempt hardened his mouth. 'You'd have to do a whole lot more than utter a few soft, despairing entreaties to make me reconsider.' His blue glance skimmed over her. 'What's it worth, Kim?' he asked, his tone silky. 'What do I get in exchange? Are you offering to warm my bed?'

'No——' The choked denial trembled on her lips. Blinking back the shimmer of tears that stung her eyes, she whispered wretchedly, 'You don't mean that. You don't know what you're saying.'

'Don't kid yourself,' he gritted. 'I know exactly what I'm saying. There's only one way you'll get Bennett off the hook. It's up to you. How badly do you want him kept out of prison?'

Her hands flew to her hot cheeks. 'I can't,' she said hoarsely. 'I can't—not like that; you can't ask me to do that.'

He shrugged. 'That's your choice. If you find the idea so distasteful, you can go and cry on Villiers's shoulder. Maybe he can buy you a fancy lawyer.'

'If you'd just let me explain——'

'I don't want to hear. You know where the door is; you can see yourself out.' He returned to the whisky bottle.

How could she love a man so completely wrong for her? The question tormented her as she entered Richard's apartment an hour later.

Greg didn't care about her; he had never had any feelings for her, other than as a substitute for Helen. He only wanted to use her, to work out his revenge on her.

Why had she let herself get trapped in this hopeless situation? Now that Helen was out of his life, his bitterness had taken over, warped him, so that he was deliberately cruel. The suggestion he had flung at her in such a cold, callous manner cut her deeply.

She wiped away the tears from her cheeks and stared out of the window of the apartment. Without Greg, life was empty, a desert, yet with him it was a tangle of thorns.

Richard phoned next day. His deep, impatient tones reached her as clearly as if he had been in the room with her, though she knew that he was still hundreds of miles away.

'I was due to arrive back in England this afternoon,' he told her, 'but these wretched flight delays are playing havoc with my schedule. Could you pick me up from the airport this evening, do you think? We could have dinner together.'

'Of course,' Kim said. 'What time? Do you want me to phone and book a table?'

'Would you? I should be back around eight. We can talk over this new deal I'm working on. I'd like to sound out some ideas.'

'Have you clinched it?' Kim asked. 'This is the one you've been after for some time, isn't it?'

'Nothing's final yet. The client seems very keen, but he wants this project under way as soon as possible, so we've got to get our act together. We don't want him to take his business elsewhere. As it is, I've already had the dickens of a job to keep him from approaching Coulter.'

Kim toyed uneasily with the telephone cable. It seemed that the rivalry between the two men was long-standing, went deeper than she had imagined, and she had been caught up in it, right in the middle. The dull ache that had settled around her heart since that last evening with Greg tightened to a gnawing pain and squeezed.

She said slowly, 'How did you manage it?'

'Oh, there are ways. Inducements of one kind or another. You needn't worry over it. Just help me to keep my client sweet by coming up with some ideas. You're familiar with all the details of the job from the notes I left you, so we should be able to work something out.'

'Let's hope so,' Kim murmured.

She took her time getting ready for the dinner date that evening, choosing a simple but beautifully styled dress in pale amber crêpe de Chine. It was a cool evening, and she slipped the matching jacket over her bare shoulders.

Socialising was the very last thing she felt like doing, but it was hardly Richard's fault that she was so miserable and out of sorts. Somehow she would have to paste over the cracks in her composure and pretend that all was well.

It was clear that he was tired from his long flight. There was a certain tautness about his features that led her to ask, 'Has it been an awful day? Would you rather I drove you straight home?'

'No, I'll be OK as soon as we get back to town. You know what it's like. Waiting around in airport lounges seems to be a perpetual hazard these days.'

Leading him towards the car, she said, 'I thought we'd go to the Waveney Hotel for our meal; I hope that's all right with you?'

'That's fine by me,' he agreed. 'It's a first-rate place. The food's excellent. I could do with a good meal. The one I had on the plane was ages ago, and tasted like plastic.'

The hotel, as it turned out, deserved its reputation for solid comfort and gourmet cuisine, and Kim felt a little of her tension dissipating as the evening wore on. The atmosphere was relaxed, the service unobtrusive, and it was less difficult than she thought to get her mind working on ideas for the proposed office complex.

'It hadn't occurred to me to combine textures in quite that way,' Richard murmured. 'It would make a considerable difference to the appearance of the frontage, and yet the cost would be minimal. I like it.' He slanted her a glance. 'You should have been in on our preliminary discussions. We'd have had the deal in the bag by now. I'm glad I took you on.'

She gave him a faint answering smile, colour rising softly along her cheekbones.

Things appeared so simple when seen through another person's eyes. He could not know what a mess her life was, how she had forfeited her chance of happiness when she opted to work for him. Her career no longer held any attraction for her. From now on, because of her foolish doubts about Greg's integrity, she was doomed to spend a lifetime in conflict with him. Whenever their paths crossed there would be friction.

She picked absently at the succulent, pink-tinged salmon on her plate. There had been so many doubts in her head about Greg, about his treatment of Steve, his attitude to Richard, yet despite that she had been unable to stop herself from loving him. And now, when she realised how wrong she had been to accuse him, it was too late. He despised her; they did not even have the bond of friendship between them.

'Are you feeling all right?' Richard's probing question brought her gaze flicking back swiftly to his anxious features.

'Oh, yes, I'm sorry. I was miles away for a moment.'

'Problems?' he persisted gently, and she gave a soft sigh.

'One or two,' she said. 'Have you thought any more about Steve? Is there anything you can do for him?'

'I haven't managed to come up with anything yet, but there's no hurry, is there? The situation isn't desperate, is it?'

'I'm afraid it is,' she muttered. 'Steve's in trouble. I told you, didn't I, that there was a cloud hanging over him? Well, now it's all blown up, and he needs to find something quickly.'

There was a pause. Then Richard said, 'You mean he's been sacked?' He shook his head. 'If that's the case, I don't want anything to do with it.'

She said urgently, 'But I'm sure he's learned a lesson—I'm so worried that my mother will take it badly——'

'Sorry, Kim, but it's no deal.' He took a swallow from his wine glass, his face shuttered, and Kim subsided, the taste of ashes in her mouth.

Richard's glance travelled beyond her to the bar where people sat having a pre-dinner drink. He put his glass down, his eyes darkening.

'That's Coulter, isn't it? Standing by the bar?'

She followed the direction of his stare, her features freezing into a blank mask. It was Greg, and Helen was with him. Even after all the trouble with Masters, he had not been able to keep away from her.

Against the roar of blood in her head, she heard Richard saying, 'He's still seeing her, then. My client almost went to him, but then I pointed out all the trouble Coulter's been having just lately—people withdrawing work, and such like. His reputation was always solid, but it won't be much longer.'

Kim said unevenly, 'You...told him that? But——' She pushed the silky fall of hair back from her cheek. Her fingers trembled slightly. 'I think it was just a...temporary difficulty,' she told him quietly. 'There's no call to doubt the quality of his work.'

Richard eyed her shrewdly. 'You're not going soft on him, are you? I thought you had more sense. Anyone can see he's involved with that woman. She's had her hooks into him for ages.'

Kim's grey eyes strayed towards Greg's tall figure. 'I...it might not be what it seems,' she murmured huskily.

'Don't fool yourself. You'll only end up hurt.'

Richard turned the conversation back to work on the office complex, and throughout the dessert course and coffee Kim made a sustained effort to keep her mind on what he was saying.

She was conscious all the time of Greg and his attractive companion talking quietly at the bar, and once, when she had glanced in that direction, she had been shocked to encounter Greg's cynical stare.

She turned away, quickly, and after a few more minutes Richard said, 'Shall we leave now? If you stay in the foyer, where it's warm, I'll bring the car around to the front entrance. Let me have your keys.'

They walked through to the reception lounge, and Kim stood by the large velvet-curtained window and waited while he went off to fetch the car. She looked broodingly out at the black, star-studded night, depression hanging like a heavy weight around her shoulders.

'Don't tell me you've lost him again?' Greg's deep voice sounded in her ear, and she swivelled round, startled, her breath catching in her throat.

'What are you doing out here?' she muttered hoarsely. 'I thought you were about to have dinner.'

'We are,' he agreed, 'in a while.' His dark gaze ran over her. 'I'm intrigued,' he went on, his tone silky, 'seeing you here with Villiers. You didn't look too happy, I must say. Why is that, I wonder? Are things not going too well?'

'Why don't you go back to your friend and mind your own business?' Kim suggested. 'I'm sure she won't like to be kept waiting.'

'You needn't concern yourself over Helen,' he said. 'What happened? Did you find that love has its limits? Did Richard turn you down as well?' His mouth tilted mockingly. 'I expect he was taken aback when you asked him to help you out of your little spot of bother. Even a lover's generosity can have its bounds. After all, it's one thing to encourage the downfall of a rival and poach his work-force, it's quite another to soil your hands in anything so sordid as lawsuits.'

'Aren't you making some rather wild assumptions?' Kim remarked stiffly. 'For a start, you can't possibly know whether or not I asked Richard for help, and what his reaction might have been.'

'It's easy enough to guess, knowing the man. But you were probably wasting your time anyway. It's highly unlikely that even his money can get Bennett out of trouble.'

The cold hostility in his tone made her flinch. He hated her, there was no doubting it, and the contemptuous lash of his words hurt her to a depth she had not believed possible. That he could think her capable of using people in such a callous, uncaring way filled her with despair.

She bit down on her lip to stop it from trembling. 'You don't know anything about my relationship with Richard,' she reminded him. 'And anyway, it's no business of yours. I don't have to answer to you for the company I keep. At least he isn't married, which is more than I can say for your friend.'

Her fingers twisted in the fabric of her skirt. 'Why don't you leave me alone, and save your attentions for your mistress? I don't need your interference, or your comments. I've apologised to you once, and now I wish I hadn't bothered. You've done nothing but insult me and throw back my personal life in my face, when you of all people shouldn't throw stones. You're hateful; I think I despise you.'

His glance raked her. 'You bring out the worst in me,' he said.

Her mouth made a bitter twist. 'That's not hard to do,' she muttered. She saw Richard walking up the steps towards the foyer, and went to meet him.

CHAPTER NINE

KIM added a generous amount of delicately scented oil to the water gushing into the bath. It was good to be back in her own flat, she reflected as she turned off the taps and stepped carefully into the tub. The workmen had gone now, and she felt an acute sense of relief to be back in her own familiar surroundings. It might not be the most luxurious of places, but it did at least represent security, and that was what she needed at the moment.

She lay back and let the warm, silken water soothe her weariness away. Too many problems seemed to crowd in on her, and there were no answers to any of them. What could she do to help her mother, and Steve—and should she continue to work for Richard?

A line etched itself into her brow as she absently studied the iridescent foam. The respect she had once held for him had begun to drain away after they'd had dinner together. She had been dismayed to find that he could stoop to blackening Greg's name with prospective clients, and now she wondered about the circumstances of his dismissal from Coulter Construction. Perhaps Greg had had good reason to let him go.

Sighing, she reached for the soap. It seemed that anxieties of one sort or another plagued her constantly, but over them all it was Greg who occupied the forefront of her mind, both day and night.

She did not know how to come to terms with her feelings for him, how to ease the heavy ache that burdened her. She loved him, but he had no time for her, and, through her doubts about him, she had destroyed even the hope of friendship. There was no way he would ever return her love. Helen was the one who occupied his thoughts, and it looked as though the affair would continue, regardless of Alan's explosion. Maybe there would be a divorce.

Climbing out of the bath, Kim towelled herself dry and slipped into her cotton robe. The doorbell rang as she was tying the belt, and for a moment she contemplated ignoring it. Who could be calling at this late hour? Then again, what if it was important—what if something had happened to her mother? It might be Steve out there. She crossed the passage, snapping on the hall light.

It was not Steve. Greg stood there, and Kim's immediate thought was to shut the door, to put up a barricade against any further hurt, but he stuck his foot against the jamb, forcing the door back against the wall with the palm of his hand.

'I don't want to see you,' Kim said. 'Go away.'

'Your manners don't improve much with age, do they?' he commented briefly as he pushed his way into the hall. 'Which is the sitting-room? Through here?' He strode into the room, and glanced around.

'Make yourself at home, why don't you?' Kim muttered sourly.

His mouth made a perfunctory smile. 'I shall. Thank you.'

She glowered at him. 'How did you know where to find me? Wouldn't you have expected me to be at Richard's apartment?'

'That thought had crossed my mind,' he said, considering her speculatively. 'But maybe you could enlighten me, Kim. Why aren't you with him?'

'What do you imagine? He threw me out, didn't he?'

'I doubt that,' Greg murmured. His blue eyes flashed over her. 'I wonder why it is that you don't give me a straight answer. Why are we playing word games?'

'Are we?' She managed to return his stare without wavering.

'I think so. I think it's something you do when you want to hide what's going on in the complicated machinations of your brain. You cover up, you prevaricate, you never come out with what's really behind your actions.'

Kim's shoulders lifted carelessly. 'That's your opinion. It's hardly my problem if you suffer from delusions. Maybe you should see someone about it.'

A fleeting smile tilted the corners of his mouth. 'You're right, I should, and that's exactly why I'm here. I've decided it's about time we talked properly about things.'

'Oh? About what?'

'New Year's Eve, to begin with.'

Kim's lashes flickered, dusting her cheeks. 'I'd rather not,' she said coolly. 'That's something I'd much prefer to forget. Let's just pretend that it never happened, shall we? Then you can go on home and leave me to get on with my life.'

'No. That idea doesn't appeal to me at all.' He studied her slender figure in the bathrobe. 'You see, it has occurred to me that things weren't exactly the way they seemed that night, and I'd really like to know just what was going on in your head when you walked out. Why, for instance, you didn't let fly at me. I said some pretty harsh things—and you took it. That isn't like you.'

Kim averted her gaze. 'I'm sure you've already come up with a reason of your own,' she muttered. 'You always think you have the answers.'

'Perhaps, at one time, I might have thought so. Believing themselves to be omniscient is an unfortunate tendency among men in the hot seat, but now I'm asking the questions, and this time I'd be glad of the truth, not just what you want me to hear.'

He moved a fraction closer to her, and warily Kim pointed out, 'It's the same thing.'

'No,' he said, 'it isn't the same at all. You told me, for instance, that you were involved with someone. You let me link your name with Villiers. Now why did you do that, I wonder?'

Kim shrugged, but it was the wrong thing to do.

'Obviously, I should have made myself clearer,' he went on. 'When I told you I have a few questions, I meant exactly that—and I really would like some answers, too.' Unexpectedly, his arm closed around her waist, tugging her towards him, and when she tried to pull away he increased the pressure, crushing her slender body to his hard masculine frame.

'What are——? I don't think——'

'That's good. Let's keep thinking out of it for a while, shall we,' he murmured, 'and work on pure instinct, instead?'

Bemused, she shook her head. 'Instinct? I don't think I follow——'

'You will. It's high time we got a few things settled, and—just as a beginning, you understand—I'd like very much to kiss you.'

Before she could argue, or gather her wits about her, Greg had taken her startled mouth with his own.

The kiss took her breath away. It tested the softness of her lips, his tongue prowling around the secret inner sweetness of her mouth until she began to tremble, her mouth yielding under the provocative, gentle assault.

She knew a deep ache of love and longing and regret. Couldn't she have this one moment, just this one? Would it be so wrong, when it would have to last her a lifetime? Hesitantly, her fingers crept up around his neck to feel the strong sinews, to absorb the silky feel of his hair.

With infinite care, his hands smoothed over the cotton robe and discovered her nakedness beneath. Desire flamed in her as his caressing hands stroked and tantalised, but the warmth of feeling was over too soon.

His head lifted, he held her away from him, and Kim felt suddenly bereft, as only his flattened palm remained, supporting her waist. She looked up at him, dazed, uncomprehending.

'What—what was all that about?' she whispered shakily.

'That...was a question,' he murmured, 'and you answered it perfectly.' He regarded her soberly. 'Now, perhaps you could tell me what you were doing at Villiers's flat.'

'I—lived there,' she said, her throat dry.

'You lived there, but you didn't live with him?'

'I...he...it's nothing to do with you; what right have you to interrogate me?' she faltered.

His hands moved on her arms. 'Why were you living at his apartment, Kim?' His voice grazed her ear, insistent, unrelenting.

'Mind your own business,' she told him, panicking, renewing her efforts to twist away as he drew her towards him.

'It is my business—I'm making it mine,' he said roughly, folding his arms around her. 'In fact, I already know the answer. You stayed at the apartment while he was away, and you came back here when the workmen finished doing up this place.'

She stared at him, her grey eyes wide. 'How—how do you know all that?'

'I asked your mother.'

Kim stiffened. 'My mother? When? I saw her this afternoon; she didn't say anything about you. When did you see her?'

'This evening. She was very forthcoming.'

Kim moved in agitation against the pressure of his restraining hands. 'You haven't upset her, have you?' she said urgently, her voice rising. 'She's not well; she has a kidney disease—you mustn't worry her. She isn't strong enough to take it.'

'Calm down. She's fine. She was only too happy to tell me about you. We had quite a conversation.'

'Steve——'

'Wasn't there.' Greg looked thoughtfully at her. 'She doesn't know that he has actually lost his job, or anything of what's happened, does she?'

Kim shuddered. 'No. She only knew that he had been suspended. He wanted to keep the rest from her. He was afraid the shock would bring on a relapse. Her illness was always in his mind . . . that's why he did everything he could to make her life easier—moving house to be nearer to the hospital, buying any labour-saving device that would help. If she can just keep her strength up, she might be able to have an operation that will make her well again. Only, he let himself get into debt, and then he didn't know which way to turn.'

Greg nodded. 'So he sold his soul,' he said reflectively. He sat down, pulling Kim with him on to the wide sofa. 'He must love her very much.'

'He does.' Her eyes clouded. 'He didn't think of it as stealing, I'm sure. He thought eventually he would make it right, but got in too deep, and then it was too late.'

'Because I found out about it and threatened legal action. Did you ask Villiers for help? Wouldn't he have paid for a good lawyer?'

'N-no. I wondered if he could find him a job, but I couldn't expect anything more of him.'

'Why not, if he means anything to you?'

'He's a friend, that's all. I wouldn't have felt . . . well, happy about asking him.'

There was a keen glint in the blue eyes that surveyed her. 'But you didn't have any qualms about going to work for him?'

'Why should I have?'

'You were contracted to work for me. Shouldn't that minor point have come under consideration?'

Hot colour suffused her cheeks. 'Perhaps.'

Greg's glance mocked her. 'Is that all? Perhaps? Don't I get any other explanation for your sudden defection to the enemy camp?'

'You had my letter of resignation,' she said bluntly. 'I said that——'

'I know what you said. I remember it very clearly. You wrote a lot of established jargon that meant absolutely nothing.'

'You accepted it at the time,' she pointed out. 'At Mike's party you didn't argue with my reasons for leaving.'

He slanted her a rueful smile. 'I believed that you had borne a grudge against me all along, and that you had finally accepted there was nothing more you could accomplish against me. I was wrong.'

'You mean I could have done more?'

The blue eyes glimmered. He shook her slightly. 'I mean that I was a fool. I took you at face value, and that was the biggest mistake I ever made. You're far too complicated to be taken so lightly.' He traced the line of her jaw with his finger, lifting her face to him. 'Why did you leave me, Kim?'

Her lungs felt tight, starved of air. 'I needed a change,' she muttered hoarsely.

'Liar,' he gibed softly. 'Let me have the truth, Kim. Why did you take off in such a hurry?'

'I didn't take off in a hurry. I went when you were away,' she protested, her voice strangled. 'Leave me alone.'

'No. I can't do that. I told you, I want to know everything. You went when I was away, so that I couldn't prevent your leaving, so that you wouldn't have to answer any awkward questions. That's the size of it, isn't it, Kim? Isn't it?'

'Stop quizzing me, damn you,' she rapped, all her pent-up emotions exploding inside her. 'Why are you here, anyway, asking me all these questions? Are you at a loose end?' She glared at him. 'I suppose Helen's out of reach again, is she? You ought to have learned a lesson by now.'

His dark brow lifted. 'What lesson would that be?' he queried mildly.

Kim's lips firmed. 'Her husband is a jealous man, hadn't you noticed? Or perhaps you don't care?'

'He has no need to be.' The quiet words shook her, and Kim stared at him in silence. He pulled her to him, disregarding her struggles, his mouth brushing the curve of her cheek, feathering along the soft outline of her mouth before she could evade him.

'Don't—please,' she said faintly, breathlessly.

'Why not?' he murmured softly, nuzzling the curve of her throat. 'You love me.'

Kim sucked air into her lungs, a soundless negation on her lips. He watched her closely, his eyes darkening. 'You won't say it, but you do. I know you do. That's why you keep running away, trying to avoid me. It took me a long while to work that one out.' His fingers stroked gently over her arms. 'Is Helen the reason you won't admit it? There's nothing between us; don't you believe me?'

Her smoke-grey eyes were dark with unhappiness. 'I'd have to be all kinds of an idiot to believe that, wouldn't I?' she said miserably. 'I saw you together, at your house; all the denials in the world can't take that fact away.'

He let out a long, silent breath. 'So that's it. That's the reason you left me. I should have guessed.' He frowned. 'Helen stayed the night, that's true enough. She was waiting for me when I arrived home from the office. She was in a bad way. Her nerves were shot to pieces with one thing and another. Alan is obsessed with his work, he always has been, and Helen is the kind of woman who needs constant attention.'

A harsh, broken note of scorn sounded in Kim's throat. She tried to move away from him, but he held on to her, drawing her against him, one hand sliding over her ribcage, curving beneath the heavy swell of her breast.

He went on, 'I tried to reason with her, to tell her that she needed to sort this out with Alan, but she was overwrought. I tried phoning him, but he wasn't at home, and I didn't feel I could let her go back to an empty house. In the end, I let her stay—in the spare room.'

'She didn't sound too overwrought when I heard her,' Kim muttered fiercely.

He grinned. 'What did you imagine had happened? A night of burning passion?' He drew her head down against his chest. 'It wasn't like that at all,' he said gently.

Kim made an inarticulate mumble into his shirt front, and he ruffled her hair, his mouth touching the vulnerable nape of her neck.

'I talked it through with her, and calmed her down, so that by the morning she was ready to go back to him and talk things over. I don't love her, Kim. We were engaged at one time, but it was a mistake—we were both too young, and now she's just a friend. Alan understands that; we've thrashed the whole thing out at last.'

Kim said huskily, 'You had dinner with her the other evening. Does Alan know about that?'

'He should do. He joined us a quarter of an hour after you left.'

She looked at him, her eyes very wide. He laughed softly. 'You can ask him if you don't believe me. Really, Kim, I'm telling you the truth. Trust me; I won't let you down, I promise.'

She drew in a long, shaky breath. She told him slowly, 'I didn't tell Alan about you and Helen.'

'I know,' he said. 'I found that out when I talked to him. I'm sorry I misjudged you. I love you, Kim. I don't ever want to hurt you.'

His mouth touched hers, tenderly possessive, and after a moment she wound her arms around him, giving herself up to the gentle persuasion of that kiss, joy radiating in a slow sunburst of heat throughout her body. A shuddery sigh escaped her as his fingers pushed aside the flimsy cotton robe and shaped her softly rounded breasts. The rose-bud peaks hardened against his teasing palms, and a wild, restless yearning invaded her, muffled, incoherent murmurings breaking on her lips.

'You do love me, Kim, don't you?' Greg said, his voice huskily intimate, his mouth drifting warmly over her cheek. 'Say it—let me hear you say it.'

'I love you,' she whispered. 'I love you.'

He groaned hoarsely, bending his head to bury his lips in the smooth valley between her breasts. 'I thought I'd never hear those words on your lips; you'll never know how much I've longed to have you say them.' His mouth sought the tight peak of her breast and captured it, his tongue curling around the pink crescent with seductive, enticing delicacy.

'I've wanted this, too,' he muttered, his voice roughened. 'I couldn't sleep at night for thinking about you, how I'd make love to you, taste you.

Imagining you with Villiers nearly drove me out of my mind.'

'There was nothing between us,' she said softly. 'Nothing like that.'

His arms tightened around her, his lips shifted, nudged the fullness of her breast, and roamed, trailing down to slide over the silken plane of her stomach.

She moved beneath him, her body arching, hungry for the unfamiliar, exquisite sensations that his lips aroused on their seeking journey. His hands travelled down over her hips, her thighs, and lingered there, his fingers playing over the satiny skin, ravishing her senses with their subtle, evocative touch.

A feverish thrill shook her body as he discovered her secret warmth, her moist inner core. Little choking sounds of pleasure trembled on her lips as his fingers teased and stroked with growing intimacy, creating erotic spirals of heat until her mind could not focus on anything but the need to have that burgeoning hunger assuaged.

'I love you,' he muttered, kissing her swiftly as he moved over her. He gazed down at her, his eyes incredibly blue, glittering with fierce desire, and then he came into her, filling her with his hard, urgent manhood. Her breath snagged at his invasion of her, her eyes widening in startled wonder. She clung to him, moving with him along the wild, tumultuous path towards that irresistible goal. As the silken, heated bands of tension broke and eddied around her, she called his name, and he shuddered convulsively, joining her in that moment of ecstasy.

He held her close, in the circle of his arms, his head resting against hers until the turbulence quieted and their breathing returned to normal.

He asked her softly, 'Will you marry me, Kim? I'll make you happy, I swear I will. I've never felt this way before. Ever since we met I've known that you belonged with me, that I had to make you mine.'

She pressed her lips to his throat. 'I will,' she murmured. 'I've been so unhappy. I don't think I could bear to live without you.'

He stroked her hair, his mouth brushed her forehead. 'Everything will work out, you'll see. We'll do whatever we can for your mother, make sure that she gets the best medical attention available. You won't have to worry any longer.'

Kim said hesitantly, 'What will happen to Steve? You won't prosecute, will you?'

He looked at her, his mouth slanted. 'How can I possibly take my father-in-law to court? My bride would never forgive me.'

'Could you——?' She broke off, chewing at her lip, and Greg sighed.

'I know what you're going to say. I suppose I'll have to find him something where he can't do any harm. Leave it with me; I'll sort it out.' He twined a lock of her hair around his finger. 'There won't be any more problems that we can't handle between us. All that matters now is our future together.'

Kim smiled up at him, her eyes shining with love. Lightly, she ran her hands beneath his shirt, exploring the smooth muscles of his chest.

He said huskily, 'If you're not careful, those hands could lead you into trouble.'

'Really?' she murmured, letting her fingers drift idly. 'What kind of trouble...?'

The truth often hurts . . .

Sometimes it heals

Critically injured in a car accident, Liz Danvers insists her family read the secret diaries she has kept for years – revealing a lifetime of courage, sacrifice and a great love. Liz knew the truth would be painful for her daughter Sage to face, as the diaries would finally explain the agonising choices that have so embittered her most cherished child.

Available now priced £4.99

W❂RLDWIDE

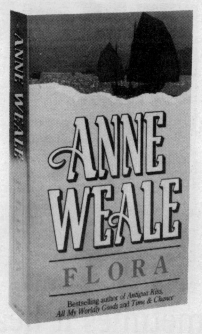

4 FREE

Romances
and 2 FREE gifts
just for you!

You can enjoy all the
heartwarming emotion of true love for FREE!
Discover the heartbreak and the happiness, the emotion
and the tenderness of the modern relationships in
Mills & Boon Romances.

We'll send you 4 captivating Romances as a special offer
from Mills & Boon Reader Service, along with the chance to
have 6 Romances delivered to your door each month.

Claim your FREE books and gifts overleaf...

An irresistible offer from Mills & Boon

Here's a personal invitation from Mills & Boon Reader Service, to become a regular reader of Romances. To welcome you, we'd like you to have 4 books, a CUDDLY TEDDY and a special MYSTERY GIFT absolutely FREE.

Then you could look forward each month to receiving 6 brand new Romances, delivered to your door, postage and packing free! Plus our free newsletter featuring author news, competitions, special offers and much more.

This invitation comes with no strings attached. You may cancel or suspend your subscription at any time, and still keep your free books and gifts.

It's so easy. Send no money now. Simply fill in the coupon below and post it to -
Reader Service, FREEPOST, PO Box 236, Croydon, Surrey CR9 9EL.

- - - - - - - - - - - **NO STAMP REQUIRED** - - - - - - - - - - -

Free Books Coupon

Yes! Please rush me my 4 free Romances and 2 free gifts! Please also reserve me a Reader Service subscription. If I decide to subscribe I can look forward to receiving 6 brand new Romances each month for just £9.60, postage and packing free. If I choose not to subscribe I shall write to you within 10 days - I can keep the books and gifts whatever I decide. I may cancel or suspend my subscription at any time. I am over 18 years of age.

Name Mrs/Miss/Ms/Mr _____ EP18R

Address _____

Postcode _____ Signature _____